Hey Mu

So nice to meet you today, and thank you

STRING BEAN STORIES

for your service. I hope you enjoy these stories. They were <u>great</u>

fun to write.

Best wishes,

Jack

STRING BEAN STORIES

Tales of the Southern Ladies Mafia

Jack R. Sparacino

Library of Congress Control Number:		2021912254
ISBN:	Hardcover	978-1-6641-8049-9
	Softcover	978-1-6641-8048-2
	eBook	978-1-6641-8047-5

To order additional copies of this book, contact:
Xlibris
844-714-8691
www.Xlibris.com
Orders@Xlibris.com
831857

CONTENTS

STRING BEAN

Carla "String Bean" D'Andrea scooted down the buckled brick sidewalk like a mouse with her tail on fire.

A five foot nine inch mouse, 140 pounds. She figured if she hustled enough, the little flame would eventually snuff itself out on damp leaves and cigarette butts. She had a business meeting to get to at 8 AM. Her third in a row this week, called by her boss. Six-one, blue eyes, wavy short brown hair singed with grey. Hank Bledsoe was one of those guys who thought his service in the Navy gave him a free pass at work. He belched orders and announced meetings that weren't productive. Or fun.

Once there were more than 10 people at these gatherings, they turned into a eulogy, acceptance speech, or a sleeping pill. Hank pumped all three rounds into his team. Twice, he referred to Carla as String Bean, a nickname no one had used around her since eighth grade. Back when looks and acting effortlessly cool were everything. Carla promised herself she wasn't going to sit through all of that baloney today. She didn't want to see baloney made, sliced, served or eaten. Especially by this guy. What a pompous jerk. His right ear stuck out way too far, like a tour bus with the door open. A toy bus with a regular size door. Maybe her eyes were starting to fool her. But three years in the Marine Corps said otherwise.

Carla never forgot some of the best officers she served with. She did her tour with the squids on the USS Indiana, one of the most advanced nuclear submarines in America's fleet. These were the boats that the Navy saw fit to equip with chefs' kitchens. Four-star hotel food was served as hazard pay in the mess. This included crab and lobster at dinner after lean pastrami Reuben sandwiches, bouillabaisse and French onion soup for lunch. Well, what was the use of going to sea without eating any seafood? She wondered if the guys on the Bounty ever ate seafood. Along with the bitter hardtack and a rare slug of rum.

Tall, lean and lynx lovely, Carla wasn't just runway ready, she was ring ready. Boxing or wrestling, you name it. Not wedding ring, not for now. Her pseudo boyfriend Brian was still trying to figure out a way to move out of his parents' house. He was charming and did look good in a suit, though, and her mother loved him. Made him chicken soup and homemade yogurt followed by veal meatloaf, garlic mashed potatoes and green beans. Finally her famous pumpkin pie with vanilla ice cream. Just to fatten him up a little.

Carla figured her career would get a boost as soon as she stopped working for Mr. Jerk at H.B. Haynes and Sons. Her marine corps training, preceded by a couple years with the CIA, had taught her many ways to kill a man. With her hands, a garrote, handgun, knife, kitchen sponge (preferably wet). Soup spoon. Tweezers. After being passed over for promotion twice at Haynes despite her excellent performance reviews, hard fought attendance award and beauty queen looks, she was stiff with anger. Her body remained nearly steady as her hoop earrings trembled. Sure, she could neutralize a man-turd pretty badly with those earrings alone, but there must be a better way. Cleaner.

Back in the Navy, the USS Indiana was her kind of ship. She displaced 8,200 tons with a beam of 34 feet. She was depth tested to 800 feet. Forward speed 25 knots. Indiana's mission length constraints were negligible, she could stay out for over three years. That's a lot of lobsters, Carla thought.

Hank received a small package at the office wrapped in wrinkled brown paper and tied with twine. He shook it gently and held it to his ear. Nothing. Maybe it was cash, a quiet bonus from the guys upstairs. Maybe it was drugs, though he hadn't been involved in that charade for two years now. Maybe it was socks. He liked LL Bean the best, even at $16 a pair. Hank opened the package like it might contain rotten eggs. He used grade school scissors to cut an exit for the package.

Carla had collected more serious accolades than Hank and he knew it. The bestselling *Seniors' Guide to the Law*, a patent for 3-D printer blocks, appearances on local television stations with CNN pending. The afternoon kind where the plastic host is a mongrel used car salesman bred with game show host. Sky blue shirt, navy blue sport coat. The glassy eyes of a stuffed owl caught over a creek at low tide.

Hank had insulted Carla once too often since he pointed out in a staff meeting that her suit jacket wasn't buttoned properly (it was, in fact) and she wore too much jewelry. This was after he had twice eyed her up and down like a side of beef at the Iowa state fair. She was vegetarian, he ate only Italian, Greek and French. He loved prosciutto, spanakopita, and escargot with fresh baked bread. All washed down with Errazuriz Estate Series Merlot 2018 Valle de Curicó. Mr. Big Shot with the big shot pallet.

Maybe he was laundering money to have that kind of budget. Carla figured his whole program needed laundering. They bumped into each other in the tiny mail room late on a Friday afternoon. Both were about ready to float into their other lives, the ones people cared about. Their quirky families, the charities they favored (she liked the Doris Day Animal Foundation). They came through the same door moments apart. She had him at "hello," her mesmerizing green eyes slicing his heart out between beats. They stared at each other like predators. Before the knives came out.

Not just any knives. He carried a Jagdkommando Tri- Dagger, she a Navy Seal SOG Tactical Knife. All weather, all purpose, all death all the time radio KILZ. Startled by her presence in such a small space and those eyes, Hank said "Hey, String Bean." "Hello yourself, Ensign." "Actually, I was a Lieutenant, Beanie. You would be well advised to pay more attention to rank around here." "Have it your way, Lieutenant Bledsoe. Is that Bledsoe as in, he bled so much from a shaving cut that he was in sick bay for a week? Am I getting close, pal?"

Carla drew her knife so quickly that he gasped. Close quarters, her weapon out first. Time to make that last call home. Actually, five minutes ago. When she slit open three letters and two packages in the time it took him to swallow, his heart rate spiked to 110. Her weight in middle school. Nobody shoved her around then. When she offered that fluorescent grin, they knew she meant it.

Someone softly knocked on the door. Hank said he thought he smelled paint thinner. The maintenance guys had been around earlier. Carla smiled. "Actually, it's a mix of gas and turpentine. They had a sale."

Hank prayed for paint thinner.

DISCOUNT RATE TO HEAVEN

Love like you've never been hurt,
dance like no one is watching,
live as though heaven is on earth.
                              - Satchel Paige

Sarah Fiedler was born in a hurry. A big, fat, blistering hurry. Her appearance telegraphed much of the message. At 32, Sarah was plain looking in everyday life, often decked out in running gear. Surfer girl out on the town pretty when she took the time to really fix herself up. This took a half hour, even on speed dial, and privacy. She chose not to lure a flock of envious parrot ladies commenting on her every motion. "You got it going on now, girl. Hey, sweetie, mind if I borrow that killer mascara? OK, well then how 'bout one of your boyfriends? If you ain't worn 'em all out yet."

Sarah's protective shield went up like the Hoover Dam whenever she strayed into public places. Too many suffocating strangers out there. Creeps. Too many ex's. She often wore black leggings, a Key West pink top and an Atlanta Braves hat over her brunette ponytail. Always facing forward, never worn backward like some desperate guys she knew. This was her business suit, her friend Marcy said. "Honey, with your tennis star build and blue sky eyes (she was thinking about CNN's Erin Burnett but couldn't come up with her name) you better carry some Mace."

Sarah grew up in Charleston, home of the worst decision in American history. The storybook pastel houses caressed dreamy aromas from all the restaurants. Slightly North of Broad made her giddy. Especially their beet salad with a glass of Pinot Noir. But nothing could ever fully sanitize Charleston from the past, its 'Hey let's start a civil war and to hell with that freak show looking president.'

Her father Joe was a successful piano tuner on King Street. He loved to make house calls, especially when the missus (as he called them all) was baking pies. Any kind of pie, but especially rhubarb. Sometimes they served him coffee, too. Alice Blankenship once brought him some Old Hennessy. Her creaky Yamaha sounded better before he started that day than when she paid him. The cognac appealed to her sense of social status. The Blankenships were one of the first families to settle in South Carolina. They made a fortune on cotton, yams, sugar cane and hogs. Sarah hardly ever thought about the hogs. Too earthy, too dirty. And sweet Jesus the smell.

She majored in English and sociology at Clemson. Her professors seemed pleasant enough and even bright, some of them, but mostly plebian. A few of them seemed downright low class, dressing like paupers. They were probably first generation French or Ukraine. God forbid Italian or Greek. Swarthy guys who used their forks left handed. Her mother, Tiffany, demurely suggested to Sarah that she avoid these barbarians between classes, unless they could help with her career. And didn't try to kiss her, except on the cheek. On a special occasion.

Sarah's first paying job after graduation was a comeuppance, cleaning restrooms in an old three story converted factory that now served as studios for local artists. Some of them were pretty good, she thought, not knowing the first thing about art. She figured that launching a painting must be like shipping out in a submarine. Total immersion. The smell of oil and turpentine wrinkling her perfect princess nose. What was she doing in a sideshow dump like this working for minimum wage? The pastels bothered her the most. They got up her nose and into her prefrontal cortex. Made her crazy, desperate to get ahead. Sometimes when she looked in the mirror she saw no face, just streaks of yellow, green, magenta.

Six months later she found a "real job." It was low level office work but it didn't smell bad and it paid her scrit-scratchy little bills. Starting with her lifeline to the stars, her window on eventual greatness. *Her phone bill.* Carrying that little iPhone around all day felt natural to Sarah. She could communicate before a clear thought coagulated in her head with her friends, parents, school mates. Posting a slick blog or two made her day.

They seemed to like her at the Amazon office. She sometimes felt like a reluctant warrior, ready to strike out like Spiderwoman but held back by her fear of rodents, men in three piece suits, bad bosses. And small dogs. They looked like weasels and nothing could be any scarier.

"Hey little weasel, why are you staring at me? I know you want to gnaw at my fingers and twist my hair into knots. Just to make me suffer."

"Let's set the record straight, lady. I'm a Yorkie. Brains, great looks, tough on rats and such. If you suffer it's your own damn fault."

"Weasel, weasel. I know good and well you're a weasel. Those eyes, those claws. You're a weasel ... Admit it."

"You're starting to get creepy, Miss Sarah. Fiedler, is it? I love chasing down feedler crabs, wahddya thinka that?"

Amazon hiccupped one summer morning. They let her go. Said she needed help, some sort of counseling. Sarah told them to get lost, that she would sic her pet weasel on them—or maybe her badger, hey th*at's* the ticket. Claw them up good, bite their ears. Turn them into a Van Gogh self-portrait. Maybe after the Oxycontin she was taking wore off and her anger pulled loose. Like a rodeo steer. A mistreated circus elephant three handfuls of peanuts short of a full bag.

Sarah stayed at home most days, alone with her phone. Fewer people were calling. Tiffany tried to reach her from Sedona, Arizona, extraterrestrial headquarters of North America. Mom sounded like aliens had her tied down. Jason Bourne was on his way but he got stuck in traffic. No one checked in on Sarah. The walls breathed. Bits of peeling paint taunted her. Sarah's head spun like a can of paint getting machine mixed at Sherwin Williams. 'Here's your primer, Miss. That'll be $25. OK, let's give you a poor princess discount, make it $23.50.' Jim looked like a plate of spaghetti with a meatball nose. 'Oh no, Jim, I want to pay full price. I'm not a pauper, you know.'

Sarah's slide into anguish, restlessness and poverty started gently, like fog slithering over the marsh. One day she had a roof over her head, the next day she was sleeping in her Toyota. Then in a friend's loft. By January, she was on the street. Her plain face fit right in, her weasely thoughts made her a spiritual beacon among her homeless peers. Her high school friend Barbara spoke kindly to her at the shelter lunch line one day. "You're no different than the rest of us, Sarah. We all got born somewhere warm and nice, we grabbed our cards hot from the dealer's hands. We all go to heaven, you know."

Sarah nodded. She would need a discount fare. No more negotiating the wrong way over a can of paint. Maybe two bucks would get her a seat in the back of the bus. Away from the driver, away from the weirdos. Away from hell.

SLINGSHOT

Carla "String Bean" D'Andrea barely got out of her law building before it went up in flames. Good old H.B. Haynes and Sons, built over 40 years and still growing, it looked like a terrorist scored a touchdown. A few of her coworkers staggered out too, but most of them broiled. Including her swaggering jerk of a boss, Hank Bledsoe. Her last words registering in Hank's dying brain were that somebody had a sale on gas and turpentine. That cocky smartass String Bean, he thought. She sprayed the stuff in the mailroom earlier. Sure did look good in the process of serving his execution papers, though. Long, lean and menacing. A dressed to kill, green eyed cutlass of a woman. What had he done to her to deserve this?

Six months after the blaze Carla was flying. Her aerospace brain calculated acceleration rates and lift curves for her career. She migrated to a new law firm, Higgins and Burke, in Charleston. Both John Higgins and Harley Burke were pioneers. They actually judged their people on performance and not their readiness for cable TV or a magazine cover. Someone whispered to her that she looked like partner material so she spiked her wardrobe with flashier items from Oscar de la Renta. The men in the firm fell over her in the hallway and heaven help them in meetings. One glance from her and they were roadkill.

Sarah Fiedler had been homeless for three months after slingshotting her way down society's immutable ladder of respectability. It was a graceless fall, full of pleading for loose change or a sandwich, maybe a decent cup of coffee. The stuff they served at the shelter tasted like it was made from dried octopus. The kind that Chinese grocers sell.

Her friend Della came to visit in the rain. Della ran GG's Bistro on the other side of town. The side where everyone had their own smokes, clean underwear every day, and a few bucks to spare. "Well you got to mix it up more, sister," she urged. "Scrape a few bucks together and take yourself out one night. Have a good time, meet some new people."

Sarah slept on that idea all week. On a good day she could panhandle ten bucks or so but needed every penny of that to eat. She tried picking a few pockets, focusing on older guys with a limp or some other obvious impairment. She was disappointed when most of them only had credit cards on them.

JJ Foley's, an Irish bar around the corner, had pitchers of beer for four dollars every Wednesday. She didn't drink beer, but Sarah thought they might give her a break on some wine. She dressed as best she knew how, fixed her hair and makeup in a Dairy Queen bathroom that smelled like air freshener and humans behaving badly. One more look in the mirror and she decided she didn't look scary, at least. Pretty, actually. Well sort of.

She figured most guys on their third or fourth drink might even look her way. Maybe one of them wouldn't be a creep, loser, child molester, or wear a MAGA hat to bed. Sarah slunk into Foley's nearly broke but hopeful. She sat down and ordered Cabernet from the cute kid behind the bar. He looked like a robot to her, spinning drinks and food to his customers on autopilot. He seemed to smile at no one. Except Sarah.

Halfway through her second glass, Sarah spotted a striking woman at the other end of the bar. Sucking in a deep breath, she slid down a few seats and glanced at her. Who the hell was this woman with the drop dead killer green eyes and athletic figure? She was dressed and done up like she fell off the cover of Elle or Bazaar and seemed so self-assured that men forgot their own names and probably whether they were wearing socks when they spoke with her for more than a minute or two. Sexism be damned, she was a man slayer. And knew it.

"Hey there, don't mean to bother you, I'm Sarah." "Hey yourself. I'm Carla, nice to meet you. What brings you into this joint?" Their conversation and mutual rapport took off instantly. Both in their early thirties, they still felt Big Ben counting down their lives somewhere. The guy in charge of hardship, joy, success and wrinkles.

After three glasses of wine and two stale pretzels, Sarah knew she was in trouble over her tab. The seven bucks she had wasn't going to cut it. She needed an off ramp, and soon. But this was too much fun to let a little cash get in the way. She burst into her slingshot to hell story, complete with the times she had to beg strangers for food near the churches in town.

"I'm wondering if a whole new gig is in order. I paint, you know. Small rural scenes in oils. They're still a little commercial and sometimes I have to match some ugly old couch for Mrs. Grimshaw or Baker. But I can also do murals, take up an entire wall in a bar or restaurant." At this point she was lying her butt off. The closest she ever got to a mural was when she watched the great Joanna Ciampa come down from Boston for a workshop. Sarah slithered into the back row and barely said a word for eight hours.

Ciampa's creativity and barely checked energy were dazzling. In between rapid brush strokes she paused for questions, then got back on her ladder to fill in more details in a vast panorama. Sarah thought that while pretty and charming, Joanna dressed like a college kid home for a garage sale. Her red headband and tattoo sleeves along with astonishing patter. "Ever wonder what a fairy looks like in the dark? What about a dog driving an old car or a jester from another century pausing to smoke his pipe and contemplate where he will time travel to next? I do that stuff in my dreams and by the way, I don't sleep much. Sometimes on a big project on a deadline I just pull some canvas together into a bed and catnap on the floor."

Carla listened in awe as Sarah etched her pain in the air. "You know, you and I could make a pretty good team. My law work creates some interesting side opportunities, if you know what I mean." Sarah was too tipsy to let that pass. "No, what do you mean?"

"I'm talking about some wet work and risk but the payoffs can be big, sister." "Define big," Sarah asked. "Oh, five to six figures. A lot more if we don't screw up. You in, Slingshot?"

Sarah forgot about her tab and the crumpled seven bucks in her pocket. She looked over at String Bean's gold Gucci purse, perfect nails and California teeth. The tiny hairs on Sarah's arms stood up, her heart raced. Her common sense took a vacation. "Sign me up. Hey, we should celebrate sometime."

"How 'bout now. Wanna make a little ruckus?"

"Sure, boss, you're not gonna get us in trouble, are you?"

"Define trouble, girlfriend."

Blow The Men Down

"Oh, blow the man down, bullies, blow the man down
Way aye blow the man down
Oh, blow the man down, bullies, blow him away
Give me some time to blow the man down!
As I was a walking down Paradise Street
Way aye blow the man down
A pretty young damsel I chanced for to meet.
Give me some time to blow the man down!"

– The Irish Rovers

Carla "String Bean" D'Andrea and Sarah "Slingshot" Fiedler wove their way on rubbery legs to Carla's sprawling condo on King Street in Charleston. The wine they'd had at JJ Foley's Irish Pub coursed through their bodies. They played kick the can along the way, booting mostly empty bottles and cans of beer up the street. Two of the bottles hit homeless men hunched over in dimly lit doorways. The women laughed at each strike like cover girl perverts. The old men barely reacted, their mouths cracked open like pecan shells.

They reached Carla's place at nine-thirty and flopped on one of the living room couches. Giddy and giggling, they took in the dreamy scent of fresh lilies that Carla had parked around her condo. The palms outside her windows sighed in content, their fronds barely moving. Feeling newly confident after months on the street, Sarah asked if Carla had any wine on hand.

"Wine here? Are you serious? My artist friend Joanna Ciampa was a sommelier for a couple years. She helped me fill up the racks over there. Plus there's some cold stuff in the fridge."

"You got anything fizzy?" Sarah asked.

"What, like sparkling rose?"

"No, like French champagne," Sarah continued. "Something from, you know, like wine country." Carla had to laugh. "Fizzy schmizzy, cutie pie. Aren't you the chick who got to Foley's with a grand total of seven bucks in her pocket? Which you owe me, by the way."

"Get lost, Miss Killer Green Eyed Baby, Madam Man Killer. Blow 'em away, right? Try to take my cash and I'll kick your ath-a-letic little ole ass. Hey, by the way, what are we doing tomorrow, and don't say Macy's so I don't look homeless."

"Yeah, no shopping," Carla said. "I've got a better idea. And in the meantime you can wear my clothes, if you don't mind looking too classy for a change."

"Jesus, what a wiseass you can be. Good thing you're funny, too."

"That's me," answered String Bean. "Here's the plan. I'll go to work at Higgens and Burke as usual and let those stupid lawyer boys drool and trip over themselves. Make a few closer acquaintances, shall we say, with some of my more promising clients. The ones we can blow by. Mow down. I'll ditch the office by seven o'clock. Then we hit Slightly North of Broad for a quick bite. Their beet salads are the best."

"Okay, so then it's like eight thirty. Then what?"

"Then we go gun shopping," said Carla. "I've got my Glock and ammo here, but you need something besides that right hook and sharp elbow of yours. Thanks for demonstrating that to me on the way over here, by the way. I'm just glad you pulled your punches."

After Carla left for work the next morning, Sarah browsed her phone for something interesting to read with her coffee and slight hangover. She found a fascinating essay by John F. Harris in Politico. *"Ambition and anxiety both gnaw at him constantly,"* the columnist Walter Lippmann wrote of President Herbert Hoover to Felix Frankfurter, a law professor and later a Supreme Court justice, as Hoover flailed during the Depression. *"He has no resiliency. And if things continue to break badly for him, I think the chances are against his being able to avoid a breakdown. When men of his temperament get to his age without ever having had real opposition, and then meet it in its most dramatic form, it's quite dangerous."*

Sarah read Harris's words over again. She sensed an angle, a strategy that she and Carla could use to make some cash. Serious cash. Guns or no guns, this guy Harris might have helped light the way for them. Target Carla's older and wealthier clients, the ones who began by gliding through school on family money or easy scholarships. She pondered the so-called "Hoovervilles" of the time shortly before FDR was elected president in 1932, when unemployment hit 25% and men stooped like stone soldiers in bread lines, bolstered by cigarettes, the glow of dawn, and hopes for their families built largely on Roosevelt's unsinkable optimism and that famous grin. She thought of her own unlikely president flailing away at the coronavirus, bragging, telling endless lies, and fighting Democrat governors along the way ("I give myself a ten. We're doing a fantastic job.") Held up by the doctors on his task force, a giant orange cotton candy capped wad of faux bravura and bullshit.

She thought of some of the guys in the back of Foley's, smug and complacent. She thought of her uncle Bert and her former lover Derek. The fat targets you knock down with a softball for a buck at traveling carnivals. The bozos, buffoons and braggarts.

Carla got home from work looking like an Olympic swimmer dressed for a Vogue spread, her electric green eyes seeming to sear holes in the drapes. Sarah had seen only seen two women in her life with such eyes, a lady their age walking her dog in Boston a couple years ago and, coincidentally, a five foot eleven professional dog walker named Katy Palmer with fluorescent blue eyes. Sweet Jesus, Sarah wondered, how in heaven does that happen to a human being? Is it a blessing or a distracting curse? Probably a blessing, but a pretty weird one. Maybe like being double jointed or having six fingers. Or being able to sing five octaves like Mariah Carey.

"Ok, Slingshot, let's hit SNOB and no wine tonight. We need to be sharp. Beet salads and maybe some halibut but no alcohol until later. A few carbs and sparkling water, Miss Fizzypants. You got it?"

"Yeah, Beanie, I got it," Sarah spat back. They were bonding the old fashioned way, tossing nicknames at each other like kids did during the Depression. Scooter, Buzzy, Mickey, Droopy, Sidewinder.

They left the restaurant and headed toward Mount Pleasant in Carla's green Ferrari. Don Lopez waited for them on his back porch, smoking the foulest pierogi cigars the south had ever endured. He still had his sleek aviator sunglasses on though it was getting dark. He swung his boots down off the railing. "Good evening ladies, how nice of you to visit me here in the sticks."

"Sticks my butt," smirked Carla. And let's quit the small talk. You got a nice light piece for my new partner here? We're not ruling out a 9mm, by the way, like a Ruger LC9, or a Sig Sauer P238."

"What, no bazookas or flamethrowers?" Don chuckled.

"Shut the hell up, Lopez," Carla said. "Just bring out what you've got and don't jerk us around. Comprendes, Señor?"

"Have a seat, Señoritas. Relax, relájese. I'll be right back."

His cat Chico stayed on the railing and hissed at them.

GREEN BANANAS

The concussive explosion shook them out of their boots. Team captain Carla "String Bean" D'Andrea had been concerned about the firepower of the explosives they chose to blow open First National Bank of Charleston's vault. Her Navy SEAL experience led her to use CL-20. She tried it with a plastic binder in a 90 to 10 ratio, which slightly reduced its explosive power to that of HMX. Still, they might have gone a tiny bit overboard.

Sarah "Slingshot" Fiedler didn't worry about anything when she teamed with Carla. Her rumpled handful of seven dollars at Foley's bar was her ticket to the big dance and she wasn't getting cold feet now. She nevertheless found herself stone deaf, hair singed, her face nicked with bits of plaster. Welcome to the big leagues, she thought, quickly regaining her composure in the rubble. She reached for her hip flask and slugged down some Bacardi and soda. It tasted great after she choked down a mouthful of grit.

Their latest addition to the hell team was the incredible Joanna Ciampa. Joanna was an artist and designer by trade, maybe the most creative and dynamic in New England. Sarah met her in Charleston during a mural painting demonstration and left the session stunned. She was so blown away that she could only stutter a few parting words. "H-holy c—c-crap, M-Miss Ciampa, you're inc-c-credible." Joanna tossed her head back and laughed. "What's your name, sister? Do you paint?" "Uh, sure, I mean not really, I just want to be a f-famous artist like you. S-some day. I'm Sarah, by the way."

Joanna burst out laughing again. "Don't try to be like me, you might hurt yourself. Better to be like *you*, kiddo. Maybe you'll end up a lot more talented anyhow." Sarah stood mesmerized by her granite self-confidence and poise. Wow, she thought, she has it all going. Smart, charming, pretty and of course supremely gifted. How does she paint a 300 square foot mural with such intricate designs without so much as a sketch to work from? Joanna painted like a feral cat, all five feet six and a hundred and fifteen pounds of her, climbing up and down her ladder while working on a large piece for a client. She often moved so quickly that her tattooed arms blurred into the mural. The cat in the hat with a brush singing scat, Sarah thought.

Joanna was their front woman. She didn't look like a bank robber or a swindler. Or a scammer. She looked like an artist, quite an easy role to play since actually was one. Carla liked her anti-glamour, her quick wit and salty language. Who would ever figure her for crimes and misdemeanors? If she could fake her way as a sommelier, with a phony command of French, Italian, and California wines, why not an innocent customer? The three ladies had mused about who among them might be their leading contender for a sequel to "Catch Me If You Can." Sure, none of them looked like Leonardo DiCaprio, but women usually get away with more bullshit than men anyhow. People seemed to want to trust women right off the bat. They had to earn a lousy reputation.

Carla, Sarah and Joanna relieved the bank of $322,000 in cash and assorted customers of decent looking jewelry from their safe deposit boxes. They howled over the word "safe." Yeah, Carla pointed out, "safe from dorks and deposited for thieves." Sarah only made out a few muffled words in their conversation after the explosion but didn't care. She was fresh off the street. Dressed like a proper lady now. Lit up by brilliance.

"I'm so glad to be finally recognized for my own skills, you guys."

"Skills like what, Slingshot?" Joanna practically yelled in her right ear. "Ripping people off? Whipping out your piece without it getting caught in your purse? Knowing not to worry about an $85 dollar glass of fizzy wine?" She roared with laughter at herself, knowing that she was taking a few liberties here. Pushing the boundaries, again.

Back in Carla's apartment, the boss said "Sounds like you two claim jumpers are ready for a bottle of Dom Pérignon. Hey, didn't you love the look on the chubby dude's face at that fancy-ass club when we paid him a couple grand for a few bottles? And the $500 tip we left looked like it sent him over a cliff. 'Oh mama, I think I'm in heaven. Three gorgeous women just bought some very pricey wine and paid me in cash. Plus they tossed in some sapphire earrings just because they thought I was cute or something.'

"By the way, let's not get too full of each other," Carla continued, "the total legitimacy of tonight's little celebration notwithstanding. We're still a bunch of green bananas. Not really ripe yet. Not really clicking. A few days on the kitchen counter away from being at our peak, y'all get me, ladies?"

"Who you calling a preening bandana chick?" Sarah burped. Carla and Joanna exploded in laughter. Carla dropped to the floor right there in the living room, her Stuart Weitzman knee boots on full display as she leaned back on her butt. Joanna pulled out a sketch pad and furiously penciled the scene. "Put that stuff down a minute, Senorita. We've gotta do some planning before we kill all the cham…."

A sniper's Army M-24 rifle bullet blasted through the window. Shattered glass shards peppered the walls and furniture. Carla's sprawl kept her out of his line of fire, but Sarah and Joanna weren't as lucky. Sarah's 'good' ear was nearly ripped off. If it weren't for Joanna's thick sketch pad, protecting her like Teddy's Roosevelt's prepared speech did when he was shot in 1912, she would have met her maker.

"Get into the bedroom closet!" Carla bellowed. "Move your fucking asses. Now!" They scrambled in like retrievers chasing down a mallard. Maybe more like Pamplona bulls barreling down the narrow streets, idiotic humans bouncing off their horns. Dozens of designer outfits on hangers and hooks tangled the trio up and muffled their frantic utterances. The smell of assorted perfumes overcame the pheromones of their stunned fear.

"Look for the trap door," Carla implored. "How can I flap more?" chirped Sarah. "Trap door. TRAP DOOR!"

Joanna scratched her way into a corner and found a small pull ring. "I think I got it, y'all." Her nimble fingers slid inside the ring and pulled up firmly at first, then hard as the door began to budge. A rickety wooden stairway, like the kind that lead to southern attics, came into view. Up wafted the smell of rotten wood, burnt cooking oil and rat droppings.

One by one the team shuffled down the stairs. The smell was making them sick. "C'mon, ladies, hurry! ¡Apúrate, ya estamos atrasados!" They heard dogs barking through the walls. Then the blasts from three more sniper rounds.

"Sounds like h-he r-r-really means business," Sarah stuttered.

"You think?" croaked Carla and Joanna in tandem. "C'mon, barked Carla. I've got a plan."

Rocket Time

"I got a girl name of Boney Maroney
She's as skinny as a stick of macaroni
Oughta see her rock and roll with her blue jeans on
She's not very <u>fat</u> just skin and bo-o-one

She's my one and only, she's my heart's desire
She's a real upsetter, she's a real live wire
Everybody turns when my baby goes by-y
She's something to see, she really catches the eye-eye-eye
-Sha NaNa

Carla "String Bean" D'Andrea had a plan alright. Phase 1 was called staying alive far below her bedroom trapdoor with her partners in crime, Sarah Fiedler and Joanna Ciampa. Phase 2 was simpler: catching the sniper threatening to grind them into sausage. Then repurposing him into fish food. The high protein snack the sharks in Charleston Harbor loved. The small bloody scraps would serve as a splendid entrée for the crabs skittering below. But *holy crap* she was getting ahead of herself. Where was the exit window she designed years ago?

She found it in, of all places, the very spot from the drawing. Ground floor with a Glock and plenty of ammo in a canvas bag nailed in three places to the sill. Crucifixion style. The Hornady One Shot gun oil smelled like perfume to her scraped nose. At least she still had a nose and it was still perfectly straight. More or less. The ding on the bridge would probably heal just fine.

First, though, they needed backup. Carla considered old Tom Trellis and Harley Newsome, both veterans of the Gulf War, both good shots and fairly reliable. When they weren't sharing a bottle of Wild Turkey. She really wanted someone younger and in better shape, though, which led her straight back to her gun dealer, Don Lopez. The ladies jumped in an Uber to Lopez's home in Mount Pleasant, just north of Charleston. As luck would have it, he was kicked back on his porch again, boots on the railing with another putrid Pierogi cigar tucked into the corner of his mouth. "Jesus, how can anyone stand that godawful smell," Joanna groaned. "Mind if I puke on the azaleas?"

"You might watch your pretty little mouth, sweetheart." Don's model slender girlfriend Melody Danforth made a dramatic appearance. At 27 she was barely more than half his age with twice his formal education and a penchant for painting impressionistic scenes inspired by Degas and Monet. Her technique was advancing rapidly and she was a quick study. A pretty five feet six and 110 pounds with sleek brown shoulder length hair and a marathon runner's build, she reminded them of French hard blues guitarist Laura Cox. She looked like she could outrun a bullet. "My name's Melody and what the hell are you punks doing here?"

"Screw you, Melody," snorted Joanna, "before I shove a paintbrush..."

"Whoa, slow down, Jo," said Carla. "You can paint *sa portrait* on canvas sometime. We need backup now, and these guys are good. Or at least they used to be. Melody also started a blues band with Don on bass. They could give us some cover. Maybe a theme song too. Let's all relax a minute."

"Not so fast, boss," said Sarah. We came in peace and this jerky bauble gives us lip. I'm gonna grab one of Jo's paintbrushes and help her stick…"

"Hold it right…" continued Carla but it was too late. Melody had ducked inside the house and returned with a Benelli M2 20 gage compact shotgun. She fired a blast to her visitors' left and half a foot over the porch railing. The explosion nearly vaporized everything within three feet of Carla and her team. They dropped to the floor nearly deaf in a hail of splinters and shards from a potted plant, a coffee table and two peace and love statuettes.

"Let it go, ladies, NOW," screamed Don. "This is my house and you're ruining my quiet time. Now settle down this *second* or you'll all get keel hauled behind my Grady-White." He paused to listen to a chorus of gasps and curses. Even pretty Melody was left flattened, her face covered in debris from the blowback from her own gun. Next time she'd use a rife, she figured. A little less collateral damage.

"Listen up, everybody, and that means you too, Chico" Carla shouted as she sought out the cat's withering gaze while he sheltered under a lounge chair. "We came here for backup. Some chicken shit sniper just tried to kill me, Sarah and Joanna. Damn near did it, too. First thing we need to know, Don, is do you know who could be behind this assault? Or maybe just the shooter's identity? We didn't get a look at him and didn't have time to pry the bullets out of my wall."

"Well la-di-da, ladies. You, too, String Bean." Carla could have quietly garroted him to keep the noise down, but she resisted. Barely. "Maybe I know the shooter, maybe I don't. Maybe we even worked together, you know, like buddies. What's it worth to you?" he chuckled. "I'm always open to collecting favors from such lovely, upstanding women." Lopez's cigar smoldering, his words stank even worse than his malicious thoughts and cesspool brain.

"Look, Don, we just held up a bank recently so we can pay you cash and you can god damn forget any other stuff."

"Oh, yeah, the one you nearly blew to kingdom come, putting four tellers, three customers, and the manager out of their misery. Not to mention destroying a landmark, $20 million building. Do I have that right?"

Melody couldn't keep quiet any longer, even though her shotgun stunt had nearly punctured everyone's eardrums. Figuring one detonation deserved another, she stood by her boyfriend's side and offered a deal. "We'll track down your shooter and neutralize him. Then put you on his boss's trail. He'll be harder to track down since he works out of Brazil most of the time. My home country. I can get you some pictures of him and his complete bio. CIA style if you like, no tracers or backwash so no one will know you have the information or his ID."

"For which we will owe you what, exactly?" asked Carla. Her fluorescent green eyes bored a hole in Lopez's greasy face.

Lopez eyed Melody like a long lost daughter. "Go on, senorita, tell them what we want. Give them a 10% family discount." He laughed so hard at his little joke that he felt a tightness in his chest and his heart pounding. She did excite him but not like this.

The pounding was no problem. Just a mortal distraction. The whoosh of an RPG caught them all by surprise for an instant before Lopez's house exploded in flames and carnage. The air smelled like sulfur, concrete and death.

Carla heard Melody scream before they both blacked out.

FULL COURT PRESS

Don Lopez's once comfortable suburban house looked and smelled like a Japanese aircraft carrier dive bombed by the US Navy off Midway Island in 1942. The air reeked. Carla, Sarah, Joanna and Melody gagged on the fetid aftermath of the RPG attack. Lopez was half buried in bricks, pipes, furniture and mortar. Carla staggered to her full five feet eight String Bean height and looked over Don's crumpled mass. His legs were a crushed mess, his eyes vacant slum lots. She pulled out her compact and held the mirror to his mouth. Nothing. She felt for his pulse. Nothing. "Adios, amigo. May God forgive your sins."

Sarah, Joanna, and Melody dragged themselves up from this alter of death. They stared at each other, dazed and confused. Each formerly lovely woman looked like she had been buried alive. None could speak clearly yet, only spit a few words.

"What the hell was that?" croaked newbie Melody, her home destroyed. Joanna Ciampa fixed her foggy gaze on the wreckage and Don's still warm corpse. Instinctively, she grabbed his $30,000 blue Rolex Submariner watch. "We got sort of bombed, ladies, and not on champagne this time. Our sniper upped his game. And signed his own death certificate. We're going to haul his greasy ass into court or the morgue. His choice. Personally I don't give a damn. He'll be burnt toast either way. Between you and me, I prefer the morgue. We can have some fun with his butt before Saint Christopher comes calling for him. Or the devil."

Carla interrupted their satanic reverie with a softly growled challenge. "We need a new plan, ladies, before the refs call the game. Maybe I don't deserve to be team captain anymore. My entrancing eyes only work on men close up. These guys are air mailing our destruction. They don't care how slick we look, they want blood. Oblivion. And blood they'll get once we regroup, reorganize and plan."

"Plan for what?" wailed Melody. "I loved that old pile of pock marks and bile. He found me as a kid in Brazil, taught me how to develop my assets, work hard, how to lean in, how to kill. Make my mark. He tried sometimes but he never killed my soul, not over all the money anyway. I'm still me, still young, and I can paint with the wind. We can always hire a new base player for the band, by the way. Someone who doesn't talk down to us. Or play us for pretty fools."

"First let's get cleaned up and order some sandwiches or something," said Carla. "I don't know what driver would pick us up looking like this, but what the hell, we'll leave him a nice tip. Sarah, would you call Palmetto Cab and tell them we have a VIP group for them. Those guys'll scramble someone out here pronto. Whoops, I think I just sounded like I was back on an aircraft carrier. Tell them whatever you want."

Sarah was a wreck but she knew how to make a phone call from the rubble. She did it back in her homeless days and she would do it now. "G-good m-morning, ah, g-good afternoon, sir. I've got a VIP group of four in Mount Pleasant and we need to go downtown. Pronto. I mean, right away. We've got an important business meeting coming up and if we're even a l-little late a huge d-deal goes d-down in flames. C-can you take us, hon?" She gave the dispatcher both addresses and thanked him with all the southern charm she could muster beneath an inch of grime. "Ah'm on it, miss, be right there," he said. Probably. Or had it been "Admonish"? No way, she thought, there wasn't any of that down here. No Amish either.

The cab showed up in fifteen minutes, clean as a cat's paw. The ladies piled in the back like filthy refugees from 9/11. At least that's what the driver said. He was blond, a little heavy, droopy eyed and young. Maybe late twenties. The wisp of a mustache he wore looked like it took him three months to grow. Pathetic, String Bean thought, why don't you either shave the damn thing off or get a decent one to stick on. Try Monty's Mustache and Massage Parlor, you bozo.

"Hey, ladies, looks like you've been working construction or something. My name's Trip Jackson. Call me Trip. Easy name to remember for a cab driver, huh?" The back seat barely grunted. He started blabbering about his years in the army's Delta Force. Carla, Sarah and Joanna sat mesmerized. Maybe this flabby dude ate his way out of the service. The army did know how to cook.

They interrupted him when he mentioned Hurricane Jane, his superior officer. "Hold on a second, Trip," said Carla. "I've heard about her. Fortyish, medium height and build, perfectly coiffed brown hair, right?" "Yep, that's her," he continued. "She's retired now, went into market research or something. Works in Connecticut somewhere, maybe New York."

"Did you know her very well, Trip? Well enough to introduce us?"

"Not especially, she was way above my pay grade, but I might be able to arrange something. What's it worth to you?"

Carla bit her lip. What a sleeze. "Fifteen hundred, cash."

"Make it two grand and we got a deal."

"Cripes, that counter offer just 'tripped' off your lips, didn't it?"

He didn't get the pun as he accelerated through traffic and headed over the Ravenel bridge.

"Yeah, I'm pretty quick, Miss... what was it?"

"Carla. Carla D'Andrea. You can drop my name if you like. She might have heard of me."

"You got it. Give me your cell and someone will be in touch." He dropped them at Carla's apartment on King Street and pocketed a hundred dollar tip. "Well thanks very much, ladies. A pleasure doing business with you. Maybe the next time I see you I won't need to spend an afternoon cleaning my cab." Carla tossed him another fifty and said "Maybe put a towel down next time."

"Or a tarp," he said, almost choking at his sterling wit.

"Whatever," Carla responded, "only next time you probably won't recognize us."

"Oh, I'll recognize your voice and that leggy build of yours, if you'll pardon me."

"Don't push it, farm boy," she said as the team headed for her elevator.

Back upstairs the women took turns in the shower. An hour and a half later they met in the living room. Joanna grabbed four Heineken bottles and settled into the couch. "Those all for you, teammate?" Sarah just couldn't resist.

Two rounds later and they were ready to discuss their next moves. The pine stand of bottles stood at attention on the coffee table.

"Here's the thing," Carla began. "We need some executive guidance. I've nearly gotten us in the obit section a couple times and I..."

String Bean's voice trailed off. Her lithe 5'8" runner's frame slumped back into the couch. Sarah and Joanna gasped and propped her back up. Those electric green eyes flashed at the ceiling before fluttering shut.

Melody's jittery fingers reached for her phone and dialed 911.

Hurricane Jane

"The wind came back with triple fury, and put out the light for the last time. They sat in company with the others in other shanties, their eyes straining against crude walls and their souls asking if He meant to measure their puny might against His. They seemed to be staring at the dark, but their eyes were watching God."

— Zora Neale Hurston,
Their Eyes Were Watching God

"911, What is your emergency?"

Melody fought to catch her breath. "Oh Jesus help us, *please*. It's our friend. I mean boss. Her name's Carla. We're in her apartment and she just passed out. She seemed fine after a couple beers and then she leaned back on the couch and went blank. We're scared she had a heart attack or something but maybe…"

"Please hold a moment…"

Melody, Sarah and Joanna's own hearts pounded like jack hammers jumping in the hands of a road repair crew. The 30-second delay seemed like an hour. When the operator came back on she took their address calmly and said she was sending an ambulance. The

String Bean squad reached for a blanket and wrapped Carla up. Her eyes were shut, her breathing uneven. Panicked witless they held hands around her. Their eyes clinked like ice cubes then melted to tears.

Seven minutes later the door shook. The pounding was intense. Joanna opened it and ushered in two huge men with a stretcher. "Hello, ma'am, I'm Jason and this is Derek. We're here for Carla." They quickly checked her breathing before strapping her in. "We're taking her to the ER at Roper Saint Francis Hospital. It's too far to MUSC. They'll take good care of her. We'll meet you there."

Derek hovered over Sarah as Jason raced to Roper. She rattled in her rig like dice in a nervous dealer's cup. "Blood pressure 145/100. Pulse 110. Pulse ox 90. Patient's name is Carla D'Andrea. D apostrophe ANDREA. Age 34. Height about 5'8, weight about 125. Breathing labored but steady. Capo Red Knight. Zorba King. We're hauling ass. Roger that. ETA five minutes."

Melody yelled "C'mon, y'all, code red! ¡Apúrate!- ¡Rápido!- ¡Date prisa!- ¡Apúrale!" They skipped the elevator and flew down the stairs, almost knocking over ancient Rodney the doorman. "Hey what's going…" he started but they were gone. Like pellets blasted from Melody's shotgun, they raced to her Mercedes, gassed and ready. The plate read UPPERUS. A snotty lingering kiss off from her younger years, not that there were many. They reached Roper endless moments after the ambulance and stormed the ER. Sarah took the lead with the first nurse she spotted.

Gail Forze had seen it all, including the pandemic tsunami, but she hadn't heard of String Bean and company. The ladies pounced on her like starving foxes on a rabbit. "Ma'am, excuse us ma'am, did you see where they took Carla D'Andrea? She just came in unconscious." "Excuse me, young ladies, but I've got six patients right now, go ahead and check at the desk." A kindly black woman in her 60's smiled up at them and said Room 20 without needing another word.

Room 20 was six doors down, just past the restroom and across from a man screaming for God to take him away. Then "morphine, *morphine!*" Sarah saw a bloody stump poking out from his sheets and kept running. They got to Carla's room and nearly knocked down the nurses' aid. "Calm down, y'all, and take a seat out there somewhere. We've got this." "Easy for you to say, you mother fucker," began Sarah before Joanna yanked her arm and told her to shut up.

Still in full panic mode, the ladies made their way to a makeshift waiting room in the ER littered with coffee cups and People magazines. They held each other in check for the longest fifteen minutes of their lives before heading back to Room 20. A young emergency doc was leaning over his patient, smears of heavy pink on his scrubs. He held them back while an aide raced in with an automated external defibrillator. Carla's response to the AED was fast. In a few seconds she opened her still electric green eyes. A whoosh filled the room as the ladies and the two men exhaled.

"Did you hear back from that cab driver we rode with? Get Jane Fleetwood's number and call her. NOW. I can't..." The attending nurse began to hush her but it wasn't necessary. Carla took a deep breath and looked around the room. Everything looked white and gauzy, like the smoke from dry ice. Another breath as she struggled to sit up, then lay back quietly.

Joanna peeled off silently and headed for the john. She pulled out her cell phone and called cab driver Trip Jackson, the one who picked them up at Don Lopez's place in Mount Pleasant after if got blown up.

"Hello, Trip? It's Joanna Ciampa, remember me from that ride we took into town the other day?"

"You the mouthy one with the tattoo sleeves and the bandanna? The one who said she was an artist or something?"

"Yeah that's me, but two of us paint. Melody does… forget it. We need a contact number for your old boss, Hurricane Jane ah, Fleetwood. Colonel Fleetwood. Give me her contact information and if it's legit you'll get your money." Something about Joanna, maybe her fierce attractiveness and sass, prompted him to look up Fleetwood's number and business address at Kirk and Winter Associates. Joanna thanked him, got his home address, and told him someone would come by later that day with the two thousand dollar payoff.

She hustled back to Room 20. Carla looked a little better with some color returning to her brave, pretty face. She had an oxygen tube and IV hookup along with a hospital gown printed with tiny flowers. Joanna thought they looked like lilies, Carla's favorite. She took it as a good omen.

Dr. Adam Backer, the attending physician, met with them just outside 20 and said "She's stable and appears strong underneath it all. We're doing her bloodwork and have her scheduled for a CT scan. She's fairly comfortable and her breathing is better. She said she hasn't felt any chest pains but is still feeling sharp pain shooting down her right leg. We're looking for any clots and will probably give her heparin just in case. You're all welcome to stay with her for a few more minutes but I suggest you go get coffee or maybe out for a walk. We'll call you with any news. Sound fair?"

The ladies waved kisses to Carla as they left. Sarah "Slingshot" Fiedler wiped a tear away. Her ankles felt like concrete. Joanna reached for her hand, called Hurricane Jane Fleetwood's office number and held her breath.

"Fleetwood."

"Hello Jane, uh Colonel. I'm Joanna Ciampa and I work for Carla D'Andrea. We got your number from a guy named Trip Jackson. Yes ma'am, that's the guy."

Joanna was getting another call. It was the hospital.

ALL HANDS ON DECK

Joanna Ciampa, the fearless muralist and designer, trembled on the phone. It may have been a first for her. She put "Hurricane" Jane Fleetwood on pause just long enough to speak with the hospital where String Bean was being treated. "She's ok now, Miss Joanna," said Nurse Forze. "She can be discharged shorty if she has a ride home."

"Colonel Fleetwood, I'm so sorry but something huge just came up. Can I call you back in a couple minutes?"

"Sure, darlin', I'll just be waiting by the phone like a cute little thang during prom season. I'm sorry, just my sense of humor. Call me back when you're ready."

Sarah "Slingshot" Fiedler and Melody Danforth met Joanna in the waiting room with grins as wide as a desert sunrise. They galloped into Room 20 like the cavalry on vacation. If they'd had a bugle, Sarah would have blown its brass brains out.

Carla was already half dressed, ready to sign the paperwork, and never looked more glorious to them. "Hey, boss, what's up?" chirped Sarah and then cried uncontrollably. They mobbed Carla and then Dr. Backer as he strolled back into the room. They fancied him the best looking, most charming guy they ever saw. "Holy crap, doc," said Sarah, "what the hell happened to her? Excuse me, is she really okay now?"

"Well, everything checked out alright," said Backer. "So we don't really have a diagnosis except for a while there she looked like it may have been PTSD. With you guys tug boating her home, she'll live to fight another day. No more beer for her for at least a few days, ok?" Sarah jumped on that. "What, not even if it's good imported stuff and she's really thirsty?" "Not quite, but nice try, Miss..." "Sarah, doctor. My friends call me Slingshot." "Just offer her water or decaf tea and some broth to start, Miss Slingshot, maybe a cup of ice cream or pudding a little later. Go slow with her for a few days."

Back at Carla's sprawling condo on King Street the team treated her like a queen. Sarah helped her pick out some pajamas and a robe. "Hey, Sling, I'm not crippled you know." Sarah grinned and looked into those electrifying green eyes. "I know, boss. Sorry about that. By the way, if you were a guy I'd ask to marry you." "You can do better than that, kiddo. People tell me I snore. And bite." They laughed like a couple of wacky cartoon characters on a Saturday morning show. "That's what muzzles are for, Carla. I'll get you a real pretty one."

Joanna slipped into the guest bedroom and got Hurricane Jane back on the phone.

"Fleetwood. Oh hello again, Joanna. Sure, we can meet briefly for coffee, what did you want to talk about? Let's keep it simple and get together in my office. Dan makes great coffee. Brings in homemade blueberry muffins sometimes, too. I'll tell him you're coming."

Dan set up the meeting for the next morning. Joanna had asked if she could bring Melody and they showed up five minutes early. "What, you're that hungry for Dan's muffins?" Her gently clanking designer jewelry and perfectly done hair convinced them they were in the right place. The lush office and fresh flowers didn't hurt either.

Joanna spotted purple orchids and an orange hibiscus on the window sill. She envisioned a slightly abstract painting. Flowers and a jester.

"What should we call you, ma'am? Colonel Fleetwood, Hurricane? What's good?"

"Miss Jane will do just fine for now. They called me that as a high school model in New York back when and I liked it. Some of my people use it here in the office."

"Ok, Miss Jane it is" Joanna began. Her beautiful yellow blouse fell well short of covering her tattoos. She took a long sip of coffee. It tasted heavenly.

"We're business women, too. Not exactly like you, but we like a good challenge and making some money while we're at it. I do fine on my own as an artist but for a really huge payday I like to team up with Carla... D'Andrea, our boss... Melody here and Sarah Fiedler. Sarah's back sort of taking care of Carla now. She just got out of the hospital and insisted we contact you. She said we needed some 'executive guidance' and figured we couldn't do any better than you.

"It sounds like maybe you've gotten yourselves into a little trouble, am I right?"

Ever candid, Joanna said "Well, almost got ourselves killed in a little, ok not so little, explosion at a bank. Some sniper guy took some shots at us at Carla's place, and then RPG'd us at Melody's house. Her sleazy boyfriend got a little dead but we think his cat may have survived and somehow so did we. We're gutsy and tough and don't mind taking a few risks but this is getting a little old, you know?"

Jane leaned back in her leather chair and looked at them like errant school children. "So you think you could use some oversight and a few new ideas, is that it? Or are you scamming me as we speak? And by the way, did anyone get killed at the bank you mentioned?"

"Oh no, not that many, Miss Jane, we're here on the level" Joanna said in a slight dodge. "We really need your help. We can pay, you know, whatever you charge." Colonel Hurricane Jane Fleetwood, now a senior vice president, laughed until her eye makeup started to run. She reached for a Kleenex.

"You guys kill me. Ooh, bad choice of words. But sure, let's talk. Tell me something about each of you, the good, bad and ugly. Don't skip *anything* important about Carla. Was it String Bean you called her? Where'd that name come from? Describe her background, especially anything military. Criminal history if any. Under the radar wet work. Her preference in weapons and explosives. Credit history. Lovers. Kids. Enemies especially."

"We're gonna need more coffee for all that..." Melody interrupted.

"What brought you all together and what the flying... excuse me, what brought you to this moment? Do I scare you a little? Some of my people secretly think I'm a creampuff to work for. I like to think of me as a steel creampuff, Captain All Hands on Deck."

They loved this hurricane woman instantly. Her poise, her wit, her attractive charm, her success, and the category 4 in-your-face blast of questions. Her flowers felt like spring and ignited their senses. Jane might be just the hell what the doctor ordered.

PLANE WRECK

Melody Danforth and Carla Ciampa hustled back to Carla "String Bean" D'Andrea's apartment breathless. They plopped on the couch, looked at each other with goggle eyes. "What's up, ladies?" began Carla. "You look like you've had too much coffee or something."

"Coffee my butt, boss," Melody shot back. "We're jacked like a cupala cowgirls at their first rodeo. This Hurricane Jane blew our socks off, see?" She showed off her bare ankles, quickly realizing she was being a dork. "It's like when we first got there I was wearing leggings."

"OK, I'm getting the idea," Carla continued. "You liked her. What happened over there? What did she tell you? Did she ask much about me? Did you give her any incriminating details about our operation, I hope the hell not? What's she like up close? What color eyes does she have? Could she help us in our work? Would you trust your children with her, if you had any? Speak. Please."

Melody inhaled to her toes. They had to get this straight the first time. She and Joanna took turns recounting their meeting. Carla and Sarah peppered them with more questions as they went along. After twenty minutes Carla said "Time out, girls. I got the picture. I'll follow up with this hurricane woman and we'll finalize a plan together. All of us, including you two cowgirl windbags. I need a beer. *Sarah?* And don't remind me what Dr. Backer said about that. Beer, please."

Sarah took her time gathering up four Heinekens and some mixed nuts. Four coasters and napkins. She checked her appearance in a reflection from the toaster. Huh. Not bad, she thought. Actually pretty good under the circumstances. She wasn't exactly sure what those were but they seemed, well, great. What have we got to lose? Yeah, famous last words. Jeez, I could really use one of these beers right now. Maybe we'll wait on the Planters. We've got enough nuts here already.

Carla continued the debrief, as she called it, with a proposal. "I think Colonel Fleetwood, this 'Hurricane Jane,' can really help us. First of all, no more near death experiences, for all of us. Second, I'll coordinate with her mostly electronically. Like Zoom or FaceTime, something remote and maybe encrypted, I don't know, jeez I'm sounding paranoid. To the outside world, it's just two colleagues and friends communicating. Once in a while we'll meet in a coffee shop. She sounds like the jelly doughnut type to me."

"We'll identify a financial target first, say two mil. Then an enterprise target, say another bank— god forbid— or art auction. Those can be worth a fortune if you grab the right pieces. Or maybe a drug cartel. No, forget that. Maybe some big box store. You ladies ever go to the Costco in town? Sarah, you must have gone there in your homeless days for the free samples. Sarah? Sarah! *Sweetheart!*"

Sarah Jean Fiedler, age 33, had laid the beers down and slumped in the faux satin wingchair. 'I'm just like this chair, you guys. Sorta pretty to look at, not all that comfortable to sit in. Stuck in one place. Squishy inside. Fake. Not really satin, not really a chair. More like a...'

"*Sarah*! Where are you? Are you ok? Talk to us, girlfriend, talk. Slingshot! *Speak!*"

"Don't yell, you can't yell like that at someone like me, floating on a pretend satin chair. Looking at a lovely Ferris wheel with little jesters in the seats. Maybe Joanna painted them. Each little fellow has his old timey pipe and their little green hats are so cute. Wait... uh-oh. There's a big ole nasty hawk on top of the wheel. He's looking down at dogs driving an antique car. Now he's plucking off the jesters and eating them. Holy mother of god they're fighting back. They're..."

Carla, the original steely Carla, remained perfectly still. "Melody, go into the bathroom and grab two Valiums. She can knock them back with her beer. But then no more beer. She'll be woozy enough. Huh? Yeah, sure, take one yourself but *someone* besides me better stay awake here."

Sarah drifted into that dreamy smile from Renoir's *Algerian Woman 1881*. Upturned gaze. Wistful, her right arm over her left shoulder. Sarah thought Carla's voice was getting less shrill, more like her friend and boss, the great String Bean. Now Mel was here with some pills. They must be vitamins. OK, down the hatch.

The other ladies stalled nervously. Melody told an off color joke and they all laughed nervously. Then she started another. "See, there were these two slime ball salesmen. Both named Eugene. Big Genie and Teeny Wienie. Not the bottle kind but..."

Sarah slowly morphed from Renoir's painting. "Thank you, ladies, for your patience. We are living in strange times. "*Strange Days,*" as the Doors used to sing. I think Carla laid out a well reasoned, structured plan we can run with. I'd support our targeting opportunities starting lower at a million dollars. Half a mil if we get desperate. No more high explosives. Small, easily concealed weapons only. I love the idea of an art auction *intervention*, shall we say. With our two painters here, Joanna and Melody, that makes sense. They know the weak spots, the dumbest auctioneers with the worst security, the fattest bidders."

The painters gulped. Carla closed her eyes and sighed. "Sarah, my darling friend Slingshot, you're back. No more Ferris wheels and little jesters. You know, I was reading somewhere, New York magazine maybe, that it's fairly normal for a person to hallucinate occasionally. See things that aren't there, hear invisible people. It's like when you dream, your brain is trying to fill in the details from uncertain or incomplete memory fragments. It comes up with these totally bizarre scenes. Sometimes you can recognize the craziness while you're dreaming and snap yourself out of it. Ever have that experience?"

Joanna and Melody sat fixated. No nine to five job, this String Bean work. Neither one wanted to jump on the hallucination thing. Sarah broke their silence.

"When you guys are working the auction, I'll film it. Undercover, of course, no huge cameras and dollies from a 1930's musical. No 42nd Street or Top Hat. No way. Although maybe we could work up to those rigs. Assuming our budget would allow it. I think I should go to film school in Los Angeles. Get embedded with a dance company. Like a spy almost. Find out if they have connections with the movie studio bigshots. I hate those guys, with their five jillion dollar suits and their diamond crusted cigarette lighters…"

"Whoa, Sarah, slow down. You're getting a little ahead of us. I'm going to get back on the phone with Hurricane Jane, uh, Ms. Fleetwood. Recalibrate our strategy a little."

Carla stared at her artists, Joanna and Melody. "Ok ladies, let's paint our way out of this one. Call that Dr. Backer from the hospital and this shrink I know, McCracken. We're not hitting up anyone until this plane wreck, our girl Slingshot, comes back again. Any questions?"

GAME CHANGE

Carla stalled for a half hour over a glass of Chardonnay before calling "Hurricane" Jane Fleetwood at her office. Her faithful secretary, Sally Corker, answered the phone.

"Colonel Fleetwood's office, this is Sally."

"Good morning, Sally. This is Carla D'Andrea. A couple friends of mine spoke with Jane recently on my behalf. They may have called me "String Bean.""

"Oh yes, Joanna and Melody, if I recall. Nice ladies, and they did refer to you as a vegetable. I mean, in a nice way. Not that you're brain dead or anything. I'll put you through."

Carla fiddled with her green jade necklace, the one that comlimented her piercing eyes. Who the hell was this Gal Friday?

"This is Jane. Well hello, Carla. I've heard a lot about you and your, ah, gang. Sounds like the southern mafia. I mean you all nearly got yourselves killed a couple of times. A bank heist where you over-dynamited the vault, something about an RPG attack on you in your gun dealer's house, and a sniper who's after you. He blasted holes in your fancy apartment and you scurried down a trap door in your closet. That sound about right? And you're thinking maybe I can provide some organizational tweaking. Redirection ideas, yes?"

Carla realized she had met her match with Jane. The tiny hairs on the back of her neck stood at attention. She poured another glass of wine, her hands trembling. A bottle of Valium beckoned on the coffee table. She reached for it and then caught herself, but only for a moment. Two pills drowned in another half glass of wine. There, better, she thought. I can handle this hotshot.

"Yeah, Jane, I mean yes Colonel, Ms. Fleetwood. I was in the navy so I'm a little off center here. Soarrry about that. Excuse me, I've had a little wine. Not my usual routine with a fellow hotshot, I mean executive. To err is human, to forgive is..."

"Relax, Carla, I come in peace. Put aside the wine. How can I help you?"

OK, girl, get it together. *Hooeey.* "Jane, we need some operational guidance and before that, some ideas on targets of opportunity. My teammates are smart, strong, beautiful women who have no real hesitation about taking on risk. We're thinking about targeting some lower profile victims, ah, suppliers. Both Joanna and Melody are artists, so we could go after art exhibits or auctions, obviously on the high end. No amateurs, no wannabes. We want to go after the high rollers in the art world. The fat guys in expensive suits with younger wives who have their nails done twice a week, their hair highlighted just so. Waxing and all that, Blotox injections."

"You mean Botox, like to get rid of wrinkles so they look like boiled white onions with Republican smiles?"

"Yeah, like *thaat*," Carla slurred. The Valiums were playing with her head and turning her tanned, toned limbs to raw squid. Live eels. Her left arm a tentacle draped in diamond bracelets. Trolled behind a tuna boat, nothing swimming could resist a strike. Yahoo, fish on!

Snap out of it, girl, *snap the hell out of it*. Get a grip, this is the majors, you teenage twit.

"Seriously, put down whatever you're drinking, girl," Jane ordered. "I get it that you're nervous. I would be too, given all the trouble you guys have dealt with. Ditch the perfect makeup, the glam, most of the jewelry. I hear you're rather stunning, and you've probably gotten away with a lot crap based on your looks. But you stand out too much. I've seen that movie, lived it actually. Some guys look past your appearance, but most can't get out of their own way. They give you every benefit of the doubt. They want to sleep with you while their feeble brains turn to mush so they turn up all their cards. That's when they're most vulnerable, actually. That's when you stab them in the heart. Pardon me, oh where are my manners. That's when you *lean in*."

"Yeah, Colonel Jane, you're right. We need to do a much better job of targeting the fat roasted goobers. Peanut heads. The guys who start slobbering over us the second we look their way. What do you think about our going after investment weenies, the thirty year olds who've got a bank of computer terminals staring them in the face with stock market data, every day, reminding them how much money they're making. Like that's what elevates them above their peers. More for me, less for you, I win."

"Yeah, the diaper boys," Jane continued. "Be careful, though, some of them are actually smart and wary. Make sure they're not married, you don't want the ones who've figured out even kindergarten stuff about women. HA! Hey what if we get together for coffee. I'd like to get a measure of you up close, see those killer green eyes of yours. Sort of take your pulse in person. I like Emma's Café on East Bay Street. How about Saturday morning, say 8:30? *Great*. See you there and don't bring any weapons. Or men. Ah, just kidding. Whatever fits in your purse is fine, except no hand grenades. I'm enough of one myself. Later, girl."

Carla spent the next two days conferring with her team. Her living room their headquarters. Complete, as always, with barely checked bursts of flowers everywhere and potted bamboo. Her two cats, Lisa and Johnny, finally came out from under the beds and couch to say hello. Lisa took the lead as usual, rubbing up against Sarah's leg and inviting her to offer a head scratch. Johnny rotated his gaze around the room before coming over to Carla. "Hey, Johnny, who's my best boy?" She grabbed him under his front legs and hauled his furry butt onto her lap. Johnny's purring could've been heard for two blocks.

Sarah's new meds seemed to be keeping her hallucinogenic thoughts under control. Her doctor started her on Risperidone and Xanax. Carla was concerned the combination might overcorrect Sarah's symptoms but left it to Dr. Wainwright. No more beer for the poor kid, though. Joanna and Melody embraced her like a sister. They rarely left her side and looked into her eyes only to see her soul bubbling like a pot of chili on low heat.

Carla arrived spot on time for coffee with the hurricane. Jane breezed in eight minutes late looking like pure star power in a classy print dress and stunning jewelry. Her Portuguese yellow gold chain link bracelet was elegant. Tasteful emerald earrings said she meant business. They set off her hazel eyes magnificently.

"Hey, you Carla? Sorry I'm late. My doorman was chatty this morning. Said he just won a hundred bucks on a scratch ticket. Have you ordered yet?"

"No, Lady Hurricane, uh Colonel Jane, I was just thinking about our phone conversation and..."

A burst of semi-automatic rifle fire detonated the coffee shop. Servers Peter and Shareze fell mangled to the floor. Three customers and the owner rose from the shattered glass and screamed for their lives.

They weren't loud enough.

BOMB SQUAD

"My three year old said she wanted to be an astronaut, and I said she had to study hard, go to college, learn a lot of science, and take a physical fitness test. She shrugged and said, "That's just 4 things." So she's basically a nonchalant motivational speaker."

- Jendziura on BuzzFeed

Carla "String Bean" D'Andrea was home in Charleston thinking about M-16 concealment and muzzle velocity. No, too much bulk and fire power for our purposes. Hurricane Jane Fleetwood advised her "southern mafia" to back off the weaponry and play things with a tad less risk. More jewelry and fewer bullets. Yeah, right, Carla thought. Let's bore ourselves to death instead. I'll go back to law full time and Joanna can go back to Boston and paint to her heart's content. "Nah," she told her cats with Sarah "Slingshot" Sanders, woozy on psychotropic prescriptions, sitting with a thousand mile stare in the wing chair. "Let's go for it."

"What if we dropped a tiny bomb on an upscale art auction. From a small plane, a two seater. Melody has connections from her days with Don Lopez, that pathetic gun runner turned corpse. Maybe she could score a couple WWII era bombs, the kind that didn't require a Norden bombsite or anything. Bet I could talk Melody into taking flying lessons and maybe that young gal we met, Skye Dunkley. Huh. Sarah, I'm gonna text Mel."

Sarah nodded and closed her eyes. Carla sent her note.

Melody Danforth called back immediately. "Hey, Boss, what've you got in mind, and don't tell me we're gonna blow up the Brooklyn Bridge or anything. What? Are you serious, Carla? OK I'll get my 'cute little butt' right over. Thanks for the compliment."

Melody breezed in the door, grabbed two Heinekens from the fridge and sat down next to Carla on the couch. "Okay, I'm all yours. Let's have it. Start by giving me an update on Sarah."

"She can hear you, by the way, she's just a little dusted by the drugs they've got her on. She'll be back in action in a couple weeks prob'ly. As for the new gig, I've got this mostly planned out. Charleston Estate Auctions, on Lansing Drive in Mount Pleasant, is having a show on October 20th. I want you to fly a small plane overhead to create a diversion. When you drop a little bomb nearby."

"I met an interesting gal the other day at Café Framboise. Black, pretty and tall. Long blonde hair. Her name is Skye Dunkley. Yeah, seriously. She's 28, smart and ambitious. Likes the idea of making serious cash and doesn't mind a little, ah, risk. The two of you'll attend Charleston Flight School. Their office is on Core Avenue. You and Skye are the same age, white and black, short and tall, both sharp as salon scissors."

Melody drained half her beer and heaved a huge belch. Carla took a lawyerly sip from a glass. They smiled at each other like two cats at a high class show in Manhattan. Their eyes locked.

"Your instructor's name is Jordan Montgomery. Older gal, grey hair. Grew up in South Boston, tough as a cheap cut of beef. Your contact in her office is Jimmy Camarota. I told him what to expect with you guys."

"Oh my god, what, that one of us bombed a bank recently and kind of accidentally killed a couple customers?" Another belch. This time Melody covered her mouth.

"Ha, not exactly. I told Jimmy you're regular choir girls looking for adventure. He said fine, just no singing when they're on the stick or even in the hangar. Makes the old fart nervous. I'll pay everything in advance, about $25,000. Just bring your drivers' licenses and dress casually. Minimal jewelry and don't show up smelling like goddam weed."

"Piece of cake, Carla. Tell me something about the plane."

"Yeah, sure. It's a Cessna 172S. Flight schools around the world say it's the easiest airplane to learn how to fly. Cruise Speed 124 knots with 75% power at 8,000 feet. Great range, 518 nautical miles. Climbs from sea level at 730 feet per minute, so not bad. Empty weight 1,663 pounds. Max useful load 895 pounds so you'll have no problem with your, ah, cargo."

"How long will this take, Boss? Learning to fly."

"Depends on you guys. Everyone learns differently. The FAA requires a minimum of 40 hours training, but the national average is about 80. CFS uses a full-motion simulator, so they can accelerate your training. Matter of fact, the FAA says some of the simulator time can count against your required flight time. If you're sharp, you can get your private pilot license in under 38 hours."

"We will be, you kidding? I'm gonna grab another beer, you want one?

"I'm good, sister. Now about the armament. Be discrete, for lack of a better word. You might be tempted to consider a 250 pound GBU-39/B Small Diameter Bomb. It's precision guided and that's great but it's a US Air Force baby and too heavy duty. They like it for a Joint Strike Fighter. Find something way smaller. Use Don Lopez's old contacts if you have to. Check the internet. Snag one at a gun show maybe, though that's probably a long shot, excuse the expression."

"Any questions?"

"Yeah, you paying for lunch while we're in school?"

"Sure, wiseass."

Sarah finished her beer and went looking for Skye Dunkley. She found her as arranged in a classy dress shop downtown, V2V on King Street. Not far from Carla's place. Skye was easy to spot even in a crowd. Taller than most shoppers, her blonde mane a dead giveaway.

"Hey, sister, I'm Melody Danforth. Your name Skye?"

Skye looked down at this white cutie pie wearing a camo jacket and jeans. "Yes, that's me. You've got guts coming in here looking like you're ready to go hunting. You'll need better boots, though, and lose the scarf."

"Thanks, I've been in desperate need of a fashion consultant. Listen, we need to talk. How bout I get us some beers at The Brick up the street. I'm pumped for one of their cheeseburgers and those great buffalo wings. Starving, actually."

"Sure, Melody, sure just gimme a minute here. This floral print number kills me. I mean, it has my name on it."

The ladies strolled up the street in the stifling heat, working up a thirst. They grabbed a table at The Brick and plopped into their seats. Ordered a Heineken and a Bud to start, their scrawny bearded server fawning over them. He smelled like new tires.

"So, Mel, can I call you Mel? We're going to take flying lessons and head off to an art auction or something?"

"Sort of, Skye. By the way, our server just reached for a Glock. I don't like the look he's giving us."

Server Steve ambled over flashing a badge and held the gun to Melody's head. "Can I have a word out back with you two lovely ladies?"

Skye stood, kicked him in the groin and then stomped on his neck. His nose gushed blood. They strolled out the back taking their beers with them.

FLIGHT RISK

"The odds against there being a bomb on a plane are a million to one, and against two bombs a million times a million to one. Next time you fly, cut the odds and take a bomb."

<u>Benny Hill</u>

Melody Danforth and "Man Crusher" Skye Dunkley waltzed back to Carla's toney condo on King Street. The detective's blood on Skye's right boot wore off by the time they got there and flopped on the huge designer couch. They had finished their beers along the way and immediately got up for more. Carla watched them closely, looking for clues to what might follow.

Melody led off. "Hey, guys, did you hear that astronomers discovered a new planet way deep in the galaxy that could be another Earth? These scientist guys think it's orbiting a star. I was reading about it in Martha Stewart Living and…"

"Hold it, Mel," Carla interrupted her protégé. "We've got other things we need to talk about. What's your deal with pilot training at Charleston Flight School? When do you start? Have you contacted the instructor, Jordan Montgomery yet? When can you have your licenses and don't tell me you found a way to get forgeries made."

Melody drained half her beer in one guzzle and let out one of her patented belches. Then another.

"You done yet sister?"

"Oh sure, boss. *Hic*. We start the day after tomorrow and yes I already met Jordan. What a crusty old broad but she seems super experienced and she likes us already."

"How so?"

"I slipped her a tip on the ponies and some weed so…"

"Jesus Joseph and Mary, are you serious? And what pray tell may have just happened in the bar you just came from? Tell me you didn't cause a ruckus."

"*Hic*. Yeah, we were all nice and quiet until our server turned out to be a cop. He pulled his Glock on us and told us to go out back with him. Skye uh, intervened and neutralized the threat. Kicked him in the crotch, which brought him down pretty hard, and then sort of stepped on his neck. He may have been bleeding pretty bad when we left."

"May have? Holy crap, Mel, you can't go around doing that. What kind of Glock was it?

"A G20. The worst. Freshly oiled, we could smell the dang stuff two tables away. He was a threat, plain and simple. I liked Skye's initiative. She's a player, Carla."

"Okay let's move on. If that guy survives we'll finish him in the hospital. I mean visit with flowers or something decent to eat. Cops like ribs and collard greens with fries. Meanwhile, get your pretty little ass through school and don't bust anybody up and don't light the hangar on fire. We're gonna need those flight school guys and I might want to recruit Jordan someday, sooner than later, know what I mean?"

Melody returned to the fridge and brought back a bottle of champagne. She skipped the Dom Perignon and grabbed the Alfred Gratien Brut Classique, practically a freebie by comparison at $70 a pop. Twenty minutes later the ladies finished it and Melody went for another. Joanna asked her to grab another beer while she was at it and the cashews.

Carla fingered some nuts and looked around at her little southern mafia. "Okay now tell me about that second Earth of Martha's. When were you thinking of taking a vacation there? Can you get bonus miles?" Her sloshy audience roared their approval. Even Sarah managed a chuckle through her sedation. Carla savored her cashews and the chuckle. God we need that sweet girl back, she thought.

Melody and Skye were aces at Charleston Flight School. Under Jordan Montgomery's tutelage, the training went by in a flash. They quickly learned basic aeromechanics, navigation, flight planning, instrument flight rules. Takeoffs and landings including emergency without power. Dealing with lousy weather, engine failure, radio malfunctions, gremlins. Jordan laughed her butt off when she talked about the gremlins, like she knew the little buggers by name. "Yeah, Corky is the trickiest. He's actually a handsome little troublemaker with a winsome smile. Holy crap, did I just say *winsome*? That's an out of date preppy word nobody knows anymore. Let's make it *charming*. Ha! Hey that's it for today, let's go grab a coupla cold ones at Hunley's Tavern. It's up Savannah Highway a bit so we can take my car. C'mon, rookies."

Hunley's was perfect. A tidy brick building with a wood paneled interior, plenty of seats at the bar. The ladies grabbed a table in the back, facing the door out of pure habit. They weren't expecting any trouble unless Server Steve had a tail on them. Nah, thought Skye, he won't be talking to anyone for a while.

Over several rounds of Bud, they blew through the Double Ranch Cheese Fries, a basket of tots, and an order of chicken tenders. Skye and Melody slipped out back for a moment to confer over a special cigarette that Melody had brought along. They decided to deputize Jordan for the auction bombing stunt. Extra set of eyes, she's in tight with the gremlins, has that great raspy laugh. She's cool.

They came back into the tavern high and tight, hungry all over again. They ordered the French dip and Hunley's Torpedo, which came packed with ham, roast beef, bacon, provolone, lettuce, tomato, and onion. Drenched in Italian dressing. The trio polished off everything and then ordered tequila shots. "We are fucking *rolling*, ladies. Let's all share a coupla secrets while that cute guy gets us another round."

The following Monday was bright and clear. Melody and Skye coordinated with Carla and Joanna about the auction heist. Melody had collected detailed information about the pieces up for sale, their owners, approximate value, and bidding order. Carla and Joanna would show up looking like anyone else in the crowd. Well off but not showy. Laid back aficionados.

Melody and Skye coordinated their timing perfectly between the airfield and the auction. They wore matching camo pants over black boots. Green t-shirts with Clemson emblazoned on the front. Jordan was right on time with their aircraft and the ladies boarded promptly. Jordan helped with their two heavy bags and joked with them that she hoped there was nothing perishable that might smell if left behind.

With Melody at the controls and Skye seated as co-pilot, the ladies took off from CFS field and went into a long oval pattern over the auction building. They elevated to 2500 feet, located their precise target, and while Melody piloting, Skye tossed out their cargo at 12:02:09. Twenty five seconds later both bombs detonated. One grazed the auction house and destroyed the adjacent upscale inn. The other bomb leveled a four story office buildings and two seven figure homes.

Nearly deafened by the explosions, Carla and Joanna scrambled around in a circle while the bidders and auctioneer careened out the rear exit. Within seconds the room cleared, except for a row of paintings. They looked around for a moment and each selected their three favorites. The wail of sirens approaching was unforgiving.

BLOWBACK

"A woman would never make a nuclear bomb. They would never make a weapon that kills – no, no. They'd make a weapon that makes you feel bad for a while."

<u>Robin Williams</u>

Carla and Joanna strolled back to Carla's condo looking like they hadn't a care in the world. Just a tattooed artist and her sleek, stunning friend carrying a few paintings. They set them down in the master bedroom, headed to the kitchen to make margaritas, and then settled into the huge $20,000 designer couch from Roche Bobois. Drinks resting on the coffee table, legs crossed, they let out cat 4 sighs and then burst out laughing. Gasping for breath, they began their debriefing.

"Jesus, Joseph and Mary," Carla finally shouted. "Did you ever imagine explosions like that? I still feel a little deaf, and frankly more than a little nervous. It sounded like those two pilots of ours blew up half of Charleston."

"I sure hope they mostly did structural damage," answered Joanna. "Abandoned buildings, empty coffee shops, a bodega or two maybe. The owners up the street taking a smoke break. Yeah, that's it."

"Keep dreaming, funny lady. You do remind me of that painting of yours, the joker pausing to rest and wondering what century to travel to next. Minus the beard of course, though that could be a disguise with you at the wheel. Those two explosions sounded like exactly what I told them *not* to do. They were supposed to use low grade bombs like the one we discussed. Not, for heaven sakes, a GBU-39/B Small Diameter Bomb or anything remotely like it. Those are for today's Air Force, nothing like we used over Germany. Get those two tomboys on the phone and tell them to get their asses over here. Now."

An hour later the duo from hell strolled through the Carla's door.

"Joanna, sweetie, get Colonel Fleetwood on the phone. Yes, Hurricane Jane. Tell her we need to talk and it's urgent. I think we may be in really deep shit this time and remember I'm still an attorney, at least until I get disbarred for all this crap."

Jane picked up the phone herself on the third ring. "Fleetwood. What was that? Seriously? Yeah, well, I have a staff meeting in 10 minutes which runs an hour. Maybe less if I hustle them through their reports. I'll come over so we can talk in private. Don't anyone talk to anyone outside Carla's apartment."

While they waited for Jane, Carla and her team sipped on Heinekens. Sarah, poor Sarah Slingshot, was still sitting motionless in the wing chair. Carla looked her in the eyes and said, "hon, are you listening to any of this? You're still on the team, you know, and I want you to hear everything we say. Can I get you anything? You're not due for your meds quite yet but I've got them ready. Would you like a Coke or something? A glass of water maybe? Do you want me to bring the cats over for you?"

Sarah smiled and asked for a diet Coke with a lemon wedge. Joanna got up to fix it for her. When she came back, Carla couldn't keep it in any longer. She upbraided Melody and Skye like she was getting into a fight with some guy in a club. "Jesus Christ, you guys, what the *hell* did you drop out of that plane? For a minute there I thought I might have a concussion but we made off with the paintings anyway. Joanna, as you well know, is held together with steel wire and her head is splitting too."

"I specifically told you guys to avoid using high intensity military bombs and you went right ahead and did it anyway. I don't know how many sirens we heard after the two explosions but it was a goddamned *cacophony*. I don't trust you anymore. Melody Danforth, you have two strikes on you now and I'm only keeping you around because I know how talented you are and I like you. Skye, you're out. Finish your beer, walk out the door, and don't let me see your black ass again or hear from you or hear about you who very possibly just got all of us a life sentence. Go on, drink up and get the fuck out."

Jane Fleetwood showed up as promised. She sat on a chair and scowled at String Bean and her dirty thieves. Then she morphed into a smile and reached into her $4,000 Gucci purse. Out came a new weapon, a Maxim 9. No ordinary handgun, the silencer was integrated into the gun, according to SilencerCo, the Utah manufacturer. Jane politely described the 9 mm semiautomatic with a 15-round magazine. The silencer gave it a distinct futuristic look. Right from a science fiction movie. "The CEO of this outfit, Josh Waldron, says this little lady is short, quiet and reliable. It can use any 9mm ammo."

Hurricane aimed the gun at Carla and continued. "I almost feel like demonstrating this Waldron special right now. Maybe not for a kill shot, that would let you off way too easily. I wouldn't give a rat's greasy back alley ass except that people have seen you and me chatting over coffee. That guy in the Auburn t-shirt may have taken a picture, we don't know that for sure."

"And pray tell, do y'all recall my *specifically* advising you not to keep blowing up the joint when you go on a mission? *That also included not blowing up a city block*! God knows how many casualties you caused, I guess we can read it in the Post and Courier! And what if we're talking multiple dead people, huh?"

"Look, here's the deal and it's not negotiable. My man friend Robbie Jackson is waiting for us on the street. I'm gonna text him and tell him to get up here. By way of introduction, it's Major Jackson, US Army retired. He's smart, tough and fair. Would have been pals with Jack Reacher if Reacher had been a real guy. He's kinda handsome, too, so you won't mind looking at him. But fair warning, don't go hitting on him. Or threatening him in any way. Or back talking. He's gonna be in charge or you can kiss your butt holes goodbye. Questions? Good. Let him in."

Robbie Jackson strode through Carla's door like he owned the place. At six foot two with hazel eyes and short cropped brown hair lightly greying, he looked like a movie star. The kind of fella that used to show up in TV westerns from the 1950's. Gunsmoke and Wyatt Earp came to mind, maybe Clint Eastwood in Wagon Train. Robbie straightened his narrow tie and put his hands in his jacket for a moment. His voice was straight out of one of those westerns.

"Good afternoon, ladies. I see that you've gotten to know Colonel Fleetwood and met her cute little 9mm silenced friend. With your kind permission of course, I'd like to show you one of mine."

Carla's living room fell silent. All except for Sarah's heavy breathing. And the cats scratching on her wing chair.

SUNK

"Those who dare to doubt the shape I'm in
Or where my life has been
Cause when it comes my time I'm gonna shed this skin
You say I'm tangled in
I hold my head high and the tides will turn
You'd be starting fires just to watch 'em burn."
- Watch 'Em Burn, Joanne Shaw Taylor

Carla D'Andrea had come a long way since sinking her outlaw gang of off-the-rails women in Charleston. Into venomous ruin. They had shot, bombed and hacksawed their way straight to the bottom of a leaky wooden barrel. The kind, Carla figured out loud back in her living room, that might have bedeviled brawny smiths in the 1880's or, more likely, 1580's. A good historical footnote for the ladies to look up, but not today. Today was to be their day to begin redemption.

"Ladies, we have entered a whole new phase of our lives. It's been fifteen years since we blew up a city block downtown so we could create a distraction. Big enough so that me and Joanna could make off with almost a million bucks worth of paintings. Ha. We thought we were hot shit. Truth is, we were criminals. Greedy, daring and savage. Charlie's Angels 3.0 on steroids. Except mostly for you, Sarah, oh Miss Slingshot. You were too delusional most of the time, remember? Seeing and hearing things that weren't there, or at least none that any of us could see or hear."

"I want us to start over, ladies. We're all pushing fifty now and though we still look pretty damn amazing, we're not showroom cars, we're more like harshly used. Sure couldn't get away with 'gently used.'"

"How 'bout seasoned, newly found children of God?" Joanna wondered.

"Where'd that come from, oh artist of the galaxies?" asked Melody, their youngest sister and still shut the barn door lovely at forty two. She still painted and played lead guitar in hard blues rock bands.

Poor Sarah remained heavily medicated but she processed every word. She was back in the luxurious wing chair in Carla's living room on King Street. The intoxicating smell of fresh flowers filled the room once again. Lilacs, iris, lily-of-the valley, and hyacinth. All four of Carla's cats slathered her lap like whipped cream on peach cobbler. She took a couple of Valiums and drowned them with half a Heineken and a generous shot of Hennessey. The beer dribbled down her chin before she could swipe it off with one of Carla's designer scarves. "Oh my dear Miss String Bean, now I see the Kleenex. I'm so sorry."

"Sarah, we have rules in my place. We use proper paper products, not clothing, to attend to our nasal needs. Know whut ah'm sayin', missy? We don't mix pills with adult beverages. We don't pass out on the furniture or puke on the carpet. We'll call for an ambulance if you start talking crazy, sweetie, know what I mean?"

"Maybe I can help us through my art," Joanna Ciampa said. "I paint for pleasure, for myself and anyone else who enjoys my work. I also had a blast getting my welder's certificate and doing renovation projects. But I'm not proud to have participated in burning things down or destroying property or... killing people, even as only an accomplice. I did my time in prison and learned a lot about myself and my fellow inmates. The junkies and psychotics, not so much. But I met a special woman who started me back on the right road, the one God offered to me all along."

"Her name's Luella, she's half white but very dark. Two grown boys, one girl. The baby. Baby Grace, she calls her. 'By her angelic grace I shall be set free to live the life I was chosen for. My sweet Gracie is my grace.' The more we got to know each other, the more we realized that each of us was the real thing. Honest, transparent even, able to see outside the boundaries, outside the walls of our confinement. In our minds, we were no longer confined. We were already free. Does that sound crazy?"

"I hear the angels talking to me," Sarah mumbled. One of Carla's cats, Samantha, circled a few times and then curled up into blissful sleep. Her purring sounded like a laptop computer recharging. Just barely there.

"Which angels, sweetie, and what are they saying?" Carla responded. "The ones floating over our heads, right here," Sarah said. "They're so beautiful, so contended. They make me want to cry. They're blue and they can fly so fast, together, like in a formation."

"Holy crap, Sarah," burst out Melody, ever the sensitive armchair psychiatrist. "You're seeing the Blue Angels? Like from the Air Force? They're performing in Dallas this week and then moving on to San Diego.

"Knock it off, Mel," barked Carla. This is my home and we all know the ground rules. No filth, no disrespect, no lies. Repeat: no disrespect. You know the torture our girl has gone through. You know she's been sick for many years, she takes her meds, she sees her shrink. Dr. Maggio."

Melody reached into her bag instinctively and felt for her Glock. She wanted to wave it around but found the strength to leave it alone and pulled out a bag of hard candy. She passed it around while they all turned their attention to Sarah. Almost like the Slingshot of old, she reached around in the bag and finally found her favorite, butterscotch.

"My Blue Angels, they've come to rescue me," Sarah continued. I know all the Navy pilots, they like me the way I am and the way I could be. We shall fly above the city, bathe in their heavenly angel energy. We'll fly past the horizon, way beyond the sunset. All around the earth before we reach for Mars. I remember in the Brad Pitt movie, *Ad Astra*, they showed an amazing airport on Mars. I need to see it. Maybe they'll have macadamia nuts for me and some iced tea. A handsome gentleman called Stephen will serve me and bless my spirit."

Carla quietly slipped her phone from her Gucci purse and dialed 911. The EMT's arrived in seven minutes and knocked on the door. Carla let them in, big guys who introduced themselves as Ben Wiley and Henry Bouchard. They brought their gurney over to Sarah and gently lifted her into it after checking her vitals. Sarah smiled at them and said, "Oh how nice, the Navy has come for me. Today's the day."

Melody finally pulled out her 19C Gen4 Glock, perhaps the best on the planet. She took direct aim at Wiley and Bouchard. "Drop her right there, boys. *And say hello to my leetle friend.*"

DOWNSHIFT

Former military cop Robbie Jackson remained standing as he upbraided String Bean's team while they shuffled uneasily on Carla's couch. Poor space cadet Sarah "Slingshot" Fiedler remained in her favorite wingchair, cuddling one of the cats in her lap. The new one, still a kitten, Miss Molly. The ladies had already nicknamed her Good Golly, a tribute to the great Little Richard who had recently passed. Sarah remained silent for the most part, responding only "Oh my gawd" occasionally. Joanna still had her Boston accent and demonstrated how they talk on the south side, or Southie as the locals call it.

"Oh my gawd, Major Jackson. How are we supposed to do all that?" Her meds were starting to metabolize more efficient lately. That was her first real utterance in a week.

"Look, you guys are all strong, young, smart, skilled and pretty. You've been hatching nothing so far but diabolical, sinister, criminal gigs. If I was back in the army I'd have busted your asses into the brig. But we're in civilized Charleston, a beautiful city that doesn't need the southern ladies' mafia terrorizing everyone. I have to admit, though, that the plane you rented to drop a couple bombs in an effort to distract everyone? At an art auction so you could do your five finger discount thing? That was pretty damn cool. *All except for drawing every fire truck* and *cop car in the city. Not to mention causing 145 casualties. Including at least 22 dead."*

"Yeah, more like 31 dead but who's counting, Major?" Melody's voice had come back and a black furor was brewing inside her. What's that old Jack Reacher expression, "Eat while you can, sleep when you can?"

"Yeah, Miss Mel, but what's your point?"

"Oh, I was just thinking. About when a guy who likes you gets to have a nice meal and then cozy up with someone really sweet for a good sleep."

"Well, Mellie darlin', that's something we can confer on, have an intel briefing. Someplace private, you know?"

Melody Bancroft Danforth stood up and walked over to MP Jackson. She had her hands demurely tucked in her housecoat, an heirloom from the 1930's, now a faded purple. "Yeah, c'mon over here. Let's have a better look at you."

"Why Major, I ratha like that lovely song I heah in yoah voice."

Melody stopped two feet from the major. She smiled the pretty smile that felled Don Lopez on first sight and right up until that RPG blew him and his house to blazes. She could smell the sulphur, plaster dust, propane leak and raw fear. She sneezed and pulled her left hand up to her mouth to wipe the mess. On the way, before even the cats could see it, she whisked out an American Derringer Model M-4 Alaskan and shot him twice in the face. The Major stumbled back into the purple drapes. Rivulets of blood drizzled down his cheeks. Melody stepped over to him and planted a 9mm slug into his heart. Then one in his brain, and a third into his liver. The room stank from death.

Carla was the first to walk over, stepping slowly over the $18,000 Persian carpet. "Mel, mother of God what have you done, you little devil? But hey, I didn't like him either. He was shitty, manipulative. Predatory. We don't like predators, do we?"

"No String Bean, I mean Carla my queen. Help me get this piece of shit out of the house. I'll need a tarp so he doesn't bleed out on the carpet, a hacksaw, and some 30 gallon lawn and leaf bags. Then some carpet sanitizer and a can of Glade floral scent."

"Sarah sweetheart, would you help your sister Melody here take out the garbage? There's a dumpster on the corner, you can use that. It's not that hot out so the smell shouldn't get too bad before the city takes it away on Tuesday."

Melody and Sarah went to work quickly. Melody was stronger so she handled the field surgery. Sarah was the anti-medic. It took them an hour and they came back sweaty from their last trip to the barrel. Melody said she was thirsty and went to grab two Heinekens. Plus a Diet coke for Slingshot. They took long swigs before heading into the shower. Melody let Sarah go first and didn't blink as the shower ran for a half hour.

Sarah emerged clean and refreshed, humming a luscious version of, "When you walk through a storm, hold your head up high, and don't be afraid of the dark. At the end of the storm there's a golden sky, and the sweet, silver song of a lark." She finished toweling off her hair on her way back to the wingchair. Miss Molly jumped back on her lap.

"Ok, ladies, nice job," said Carla. My CIA guys can keep the heat off us for maybe a week or so. *Maybe*. So I'm just wondering one small detail."

Silence echoed from Slingshot, Joanna, and Melody as they fiddled with their drinks and Miss Molly. The other cats stayed under the couch.

"Then what?"

Get Up and Dance

"*Old pirates, yes, they rob*
Sold I to the merchant ships
Minutes after they took
From the bottomless pit
Emancipate yourselves from mental slavery
None but ourselves can free our minds
Have no fear for atomic energy
'Cause none of them can stop the time"
         - Redemption Song, Bob Marley

Carla sprang at Melody like a cougar. She tackled her hard, like they taught her as a Navy Seal. Melody went down backwards, cracking her skull on the maple end table. Her Glock bounced off the hardwood floor and went off in a concussive explosion. The two stunned EMT's she had intended it for gagged on their adrenaline blast.

String Bean pinned her down while Ben and Henry rushed over to check her vitals. A worm of bubbling blood slid down Melody's mouth, her blue eyes shining like cracked sapphire. Mighty Mel, the Mistress of Mean, trembled just enough to signal she was still alive.

Carla only meant to temporarily disable her, not create an invalid destined for weeks in traction, eating broth and Jell-O. The men made a quick decision. Ben hung over Melody and fed her oxygen. Henry grabbed his phone from his belt.

"Yeah, this is Chico 10, we're at 25 Kingston Street with a barely conscious woman. Caucasian, maybe 40, slim build. She was just kick-ass tackled by another woman here, a Carla… what is it, ma'am?… D'Andrea. The condo owner. Banged her head on a table. Bleeding pretty bad from the mouth, can't speak or move. We're taking her in. ETA seven minutes. Send a crew back here to look at another woman who may be hallucinating. Over."

Their stretcher already there, the men made quick work of gently lifting Melody off the deck and strapping her in. Both paramedics, they jabbed her with 20 mg of morphine and headed back to the ambulance. Their siren wailed through the mist as they headed to the Neuroscience ICU at MUSC.

Carla and her team sat in tears, staring at each other with astonishment. Joanna spoke first, rising slowly to her feet after downing a hefty shot of Hennessy. She let out a deep breath, and quoted from memory, Peter 3:3-4 MSG.

"What matters is not your outward appearance—the styling of your hair, the jewelry you wear, the cut of your clothes—but your inner disposition. Cultivate inner beauty, the gentle, gracious kind that God delights in."

"Come on, ladies. We can do a lot better. We've got all the tools and then some. Brains, beauty, talent, ferocity."

Carla took the bait. "So the hell what, Jo? Now what do we do? And while you're thinking about that, how bout pouring me some of that Hennessy. My throat is pretty damn dry, sweetie."

Poor Sarah, poor little Slingshot, rocked quietly in her favorite wingchair. She began to softly hum the heavenly aria, "O mio babbino caro" from Puccini's *Gianni Schicchi*. Carla jumped on her phone to locate the orchestral version and let her sing. Sarah's eyes opened for a few seconds and then closed in complete bliss. The speaker system swept them to Italy, Sarah's luscious soprano sweeping them far away. The cats purred softly, the explosion of fresh flowers bowed their heads. Joanna wept from her soul, her heart soaring on a whiff of lilacs and honeysuckle.

Ever the team leader, Carla detonated their reverie. She pulled her 5'8" leggy frame to attention in a blowtorch of redirection.

"Ladies, ladies, please! We need to go the hospital and check on our girl. We're trading one lovely melody for our sister Melody. C'mon, let's go! Andiamo Andiamo! We can sing later, maybe we can dance. Move it, girls!"

Carla briefly considered calling her neighbor Sandy to come watch over Sarah while they went to the hospital. The thought vaporized in the time it took to appear. Carla and Joanna eased over to Sarah and asked her if she was good to go. Sarah shifted two cats off her lap and nodded.

"Can I go like this, in my bathrobe?"

Carla knew that was coming and looked to Joanna. In seconds Joanna returned from the guest bathroom with a pretty flower print dress and a floppy straw hat. "Here, Sling, just drop your robe and slip this on. Remember when you picked it out last week?"

Sarah "Slingshot" Fiedler flicked away the hat, put on the dress, and grabbed a Clemson ball cap from her bathrobe pocket. "I'm ready, guys, how do I look? Like normal or still like batshit crazy lady?"

Carla and Joanna gently held her by each elbow and walked her to the door. By the time they reached the street Carla's new Mercedes was waiting. "Howja do that, boss?"

"Magic, girl. Everyone get in. Buckle up cuz we're gonna fly."

The gang hit the hospital in ten minutes, their hearts on fire, their cheeks flush with anxiety. Carla and Joanna blew through the checkpoints and got them all to Melody's room in the time it takes a thief to pocket a Rolex off a drunken convention goer. Melody looked up at them like she was stoned. She was stoned, on Dilaudid. An IV drip snaked into her left arm. A way too young doctor quickly intercepted them.

"Hello, ladies, welcome aboard. I'm Doctor Morris. Everyone calls me Doctor Wayne. Please don't plan to stay here long, this young woman suffered a very serious neurological trauma. Not to mention a couple of cracked vertebrae. She'll probably recover pretty well and we have her on pain meds and some rehydration. Good thing she was in pretty good shape to begin with, that was some combination of blows she suffered. I'll be back in a few minutes to see Melody. Alone. Okay?"

Resisting competing urges to kick him in the groin and hug him to death, Joanna bit her tongue and smiled that man killer smile. She let her tattoo sleeves and steel melting smile do her talking. Carla offered a "Sure, Dr. Morris, we'll be long gone. Promise."

Morris slipped out of the room and padded down the hall with his clipboard and a cellphone hanging out of his scrubs. He walked like Kevin Costner after a couple of beers.

"Okay, quick, you guys, we gotta work fast. Get into her heart and head. Shoot her up with music. What've we got, Jo?"

Joanna reached for her cell and put on Samantha Fish performing "Gone for Good" in Telleride, Colorado, an enchanting setting snugged up against San Juan tuck of the Rockies.

> *Well, I'm not the kind of company you're, you're accustomed to*
> *You've got such a calmness that, I, I can't break on through*
> *Did everything you wanted me to, to make you stay*
> *Every reason lordy was just an excuse, you know*
> *He was a perfect getaway*

Melody's eyes opened like steamed oysters. Sarah said she thought she saw pearls. Melody started to sway to the blues rock classic, then shifted in her bed and tried to get up.

"Oh, man, I'm flying. I wanna dance to this music. Sam Fish, right?"

Joanna began to dance in place. Sarah followed, then Carla. They had their girl back. She was going to make it.

Dr. Wayne walked in on their reverie. Only Sarah thought he was smiling.

Helldivers

*"**Grebe**, (order Podicipediformes), are best known for the striking courtship displays of some species and for the silky <u>plumage</u> of the underparts, which formerly was much used in millinery. The speed with which grebes can submerge has earned them such names as water-witch and helldiver, while the position of the feet near the tail is responsible for the early English name arsefoot, from which the <u>family name</u> was derived."*

- Britannica

"It sent Japanese warships to the bottom of the ocean. It pulverized fortifications on Japan's home islands. The Curtiss SB2C Helldiver dive-bomber left a trail of wreckage in its wake, the debris and detritus of a devastated foe. Yet, the Helldiver is remembered today mostly as an unpopular latecomer to the war, a less than stellar performer built by an aircraft company in decline."

— Warfarehistorynetwork.com

Melody Danforth, the most aggressive and daring of the String Bean southern mafia, came back from the hospital to Carla's Charleston condo on a glorious Saturday afternoon. She loved her boss with all her heart and felt eternally grateful for her reprieve. The graceful palm trees along King Street waved her a kind welcome. A lone gull saluted overhead on a light easterly breeze. The smell of gardenias filled Melody's lungs. Home again, she was back in her nest.

Carla "String Bean" D'Andrea started the rotors in her military helicopter brain and asked her newly hired executive assistant Brandy Jackson to fetch a round of drinks for everyone, then asked her to find a seat and join them. Tiny blonde Brandy grabbed a fistful of Heinekens from a silver goblet, so cold they felt frozen, a flask of Johnny Walker Black scotch, glasses and a bowl of mixed nuts. She carefully arranged them on a gigantic tray and strolled carefully into the living room. The ladies poured their beers to get the proper heads and joined in a toast.

"Melody, this 'Bud's' for you, sweetie," Carla began. "We are ecstatic to have you back from the dead and I apologize for tackling you so hard. Yes, I prevented you from committing homicide on that poor EMT in my living room, but I let my adrenaline push me a tiny bit over the top. I never meant to catapult you into the hospital, just to disable you. I am truly sorry I hurt you so badly."

The ladies murmured amen and you go girl. They drained their icy beers in the time it takes a mosquito to draw blood. Joanna tilted her head back and let out a truck driver quality belch. They all howled with laughter, tears flooding their cheeks. Even psychological wreck Sarah joined in the chorus. They refilled their glasses with another tray of beer that Brandy brought in without a word from Carla. Again they chugged away like freight trains. Again the gale of sisterly laughter filled the room. A round of scotch later they settled in for Carla's announcement.

"Ladies, I am beyond delighted to have you here again today. It has been far too long. First of all, I've stayed in contact with Hurricane Jane and she's offered some good ideas for us to consider in terms of how, and frankly if, we go forward. I also planned a bit of a surprise for us today. I'm about to introduce you to an amazing woman about our age with a fascinating background. Her name is Michelle." Carla picked up her phone and hit speed dial. A minute later there was a gentle knock on the door. Everyone looked over at it as Brandy rose to answer.

Michelle strode in with the confidence of a runway model. She was blowout pretty with shoulder length blonde hair, five foot eight and maybe 125 pounds counting her clothes, shoes, and designer handbag. Carla welcomed her with a hug and invited her to sit on the couch. Joanna, Sarah Melody and Brandy looked on eagerly. They had no idea what was coming but the alcohol coursing through them fueled an optimism they hadn't felt together in years.

Michelle lay down her purse, looked around the room and paused for a long moment. Her Mona Lisa smile bloomed into a broad grin.

Only Joanna continued to sip her scotch. The clink of ice cubes ricocheted around the room.

Finally, Michelle spoke. "Thank you for inviting me into your sanctuary and please excuse my accent. I am Michelle Petrov. I was born in Peoria, Illinois but raised in Bulgaria. My father was an engineer and most of his business was in Sofia, the capital. He accumulated great wealth before passing away last year. My mother died the year before. The doctors said it was heart disease but I don't trust the medical system over there. Or anything else I was taught growing up, especially about America.

Charleston is an amazing city. I was here on a photo shoot when the director wouldn't stop hitting on me. I escaped into a local bar to get away from him and met Carla. I guess like Sarah many years ago, I was mesmerized by String Bean, as you call her. We're about the same height and she should have been the one in the photo shoot, not me. She's just more dazzling than me. I'm just a regular girl from Europe. Nothing special."

"Go on, Michelle," Joanna said. "We're all ears." All eyes stayed on Michelle. Carla and her gang were mesmerized and drunk. They sat in a wax museum of awe and admiration. No one dared to speak. Only the sound of Brandy working back in the kitchen broke the silence.

Michelle stood up, her drink shaking in her hand. Tears flowed down her cheeks. Carla had put on Mozart, playing quietly in the background.

"I have a proposal for you. I want to help you achieve redemption and we can start in several ways. One is to reconnect with nature and another is to find God again. I think we can do both, maybe if we head up to Boston. I went there last year. The harbor is lovely, overlooking the Prudential Center and the John Hancock building and the University. We can take a trip there and just sit along the harbor. Maybe take some lunch. We can watch the helldivers as they fish for menhaden and other bait. They're ferocious hunters but they only do that to eat and sustain themselves. This is very different from your behavior over the years. I don't wish to make judgments but there's a better path for you. And for me."

The sound of Mozart's *The Magic Flute* surrounded the women and deepened their intoxication. Carla asked Joanna to get on the phone and make reservations for the best hotel in Boston and flight arrangements. Joanna proceeded without blinking. She loved Carla with a frightening intensity. Sometimes it truly scared her.

Carla took over the meeting again. She stood up to her to her full fashion model height and cleared her throat. She leaned over to put down her drink and then paused. "Brandy? Brandy! What are you doing out there? I smell something strange. Like rotten eggs or something. Tell me you're making something weird for us and tell me now. If you're not we may be in real trouble." Carla knew that smell. It was hydrogen sulfide, poisonous and explosive. Those bastards were after them again. Had to be the same assholes from years ago who tried to shoot them and bomb them. Just logically had to be them.

"Everybody out and I mean *right now*! We've to get out of here *immediately*. That funny smell is poison. It's going to explode. Get out of this goddamn apartment or I will shoot you right here. Get out. *Get the hell out!*"

The ladies raced out the door dragging Brandy with them. Sarah in the rear, glued to Melody's arm. Barefoot carrying one of the cats. The explosion launched them into the street. Carla and Brandy crashed into parked cars. Sarah and Melody collided with them in a heap. Joanna got back on her phone. She could taste her own terror.

BEANTOWN BIRDS

"...Abigail's singing while I painted. How we laughed so when no one was watching. And how finding a black-eyed Susan tucked into my business contracts reminded me of why I was doing that business in the first place. To really care for another is a reason to live."

- Adriana Mather, *How to Hang a Witch*

"Excellent teachers showered on to us like meteors: Biology teachers holding up human brains, English teachers inspiring us with a personal ideological fierceness about Tolstoy and Plato, Art teachers leading us through the slums of Boston, then back to the easel to hurl public school gouache with social awareness and fury."

- Sylvia Plath

Carla, Joanna, Melody, Sarah, Michelle and Brandy hit Charleston International Airport with a fury born of desperation. They hadn't time to pack anything after the explosion that blasted them onto King Street outside Carla's plush condo. Not a bag, not a purse, not a bag of peanuts. No weapons except for a 3D printer handgun that Mighty Mel stuffed down her Clemson sweatshirt. Joanna and Carla had their phones, still intact from the detonation and stayed on them to United's Gate 3. Brandy had a wad of hundreds in her jacket pocket and instinctively hustled to the nearest bar and gift shop. She talked the scrawny kid bartender into selling her three bottles of chilled Chardonnay and a sack of cold Coors Light. Hustling over to the gate she fought off strange stares. A quick stop for snacks left her burdened down but more determined than ever to hurry back to her "family."

The flight to Boston in business class was bumpy but tolerable. They stayed together, still buzzed from the wine when the steward came around offering drinks. They ordered double scotches and a round of beer. Their 757 finally left the turbulence behind and the captain thanked them for their patience and assured them the remainder of the flight looked to be smooth and uneventful. Their steward, Donnie Mae, thought they were funny and couldn't resist joining the banter.

Captain Ron Jacobs, with 30,000 flight hours under his belt, eased the jet into Boston's Logan Airport. Joanna and Brandy double teamed on hotel reservations and booked the gang into the Four Seasons on Boylston Street. Joanna then called for an Uber van so they could stretch out on the way to the hotel. As Carla looked around, it was hard to tell who was more inebriated, including herself. She handed a beer to a homeless guy who looked like he had been sleeping in a trash heap for a week. His eyes fluttered for a moment and his lips trembled as he thanked her. String Bean was sympathetic but she had no trouble resisting the urge to give him a hug. The word vermin came to mind.

Their dark gray van arrived in minutes and they got to the hotel in what felt like minutes. They checked in and headed up to their three suites. Carla and her lieutenant Joanna took one, Melody and Brandy took one next door. Sarah grew nervous with staying with newcomer Michelle and asked to join Mel and Brandy.

"That sounds like a party," chirped Melody. "Just so that you know, I snore. Don't go flipping out about that later, sister."

Brandy ordered dinner for the team, who headquartered with Carla. She set up a dinner table and whistled over the other ladies just before the food and two bottles of champagne with crystal stems arrived. Lobster, broccoli ravioli with oyster mushrooms, arborio rice and Caesar salads. A stunning platter of art décor sushi riveted their attention.

Carla raised her glass in a triumphant toast. "Ashes to ashes, dust to dust, and quartz to gold. We made it. We goddamn made it. We're divers, ladies, hell divers. We dove out of my condo in front of that gas blast. We dove into a flight to a city 1,000 miles away, and we dove into this joint. Actually I think it ain't too terrible, waddya you guys think?"

The ladies roared with laughter. They were on vacation at last. They were on sabbatical, long overdue. Carla presided proudly over a sloshy dinner. The ladies ate like wolves. Their laughter shook the suite. Poor hallucinating Sarah passed out first. Then the rest until only Joanna was left standing. She forced herself to stagger into the bathroom. Squatted on the toilet and drifted off. Carla found her in the morning, smiling and still drunk. She made French press coffee for them and led her back to the living room. The others were strewn about like dolls. Still dressed, still in their shoes. Still dreaming. She thought about girls just wanting to have fun. How could that be bad?

Room service brought them a huge platter of steak and eggs, cut fruit, muffins, and coffee in a silver pitcher. Michelle led them in an ancient Creole song, a prayer she felt they could share. She closed her eyes and sang in a soft, trained soprano from her soul.

God will make a way,
God will make a way, Where there seems to be no way.
He Works in ways we cannot see
He will make a way, he will make a way
He will be my guide,
Hold me closely to his side.

She paused to look around the suite. Carla's gang, her southern mafia, had put down their forks in solemn recognition of a transformational moment. Michelle began the song from the top and they began to sing along. Sparrows chirped outside their windows. The sun played tag with huge cumulous clouds. Carla bowed her head. Joanna followed immediately, then Melody, Sarah and Brandy. They had bonded in song and a commitment to redeem themselves before God.

After a thirty minute ride in another huge Uber van they descended on Marina Bay in North Quincy. Brandy ducked into the small market with a credit card that Carla always kept on her. She emerged in minutes with chilled bottles of champagne. They found benches near the Reel House restaurant and borrowed glasses from a server. They promised her that they would get a table and order from the menu soon. And what a menu. Lobster rolls, fried calamari, grilled cheeseburgers to die for, eighteen kinds of draft beer and lo and behold, margaritas and something called a "hangover buster." But first the birds. They had to watch the sea birds.

Random splashes below in the harbor, spitting distance from the lovely boats, suggested that a mega baitfish, menhaden, hunted underneath. Three helldivers crash landed into the water. Shook their heads and seemed to check their feathers and beaks. Time to hunt.

The first grebe to dive had a white streak behind its head. They named her Kiki. She stayed under for over half a minute, finally surfacing fifty yards away. She cinched a silver fish in her mouth, still struggling. Three quick head jerks and the fish went down head first into Kiki's gullet. She dove back down. "They really love sushi, don't they?" asked Sarah. She was with them now, they could feel it. They loved Sarah like an injured animal. Carla thought a fawn, Joanna a puppy. They also loved her as their sister, their flesh.

The other helldivers headed for the bottom of the harbor. The ladies watched them for hours before turning around to face the enticing row of restaurants. They all wanted seafood. Preferably sushi.

BENEDICTION

"The path of meditation and the paths of our lives together has to do with curiosity, inquisitiveness. The ground is ourselves; we are here to study ourselves and to get to know ourselves now, not later."

\- Awakening Loving-Kindness, Pema Chodron

Back at the Four Seasons, the ladies moved into Carla's glorious suite, their headquarters on the road. They curled around her wing chair, the queen on her throne. She brushed a few strands of hair from her eyes and looked around the room. Ice melting in the silver bucket was the only sound.

Joanna was the first to speak. She cleared her throat and began quietly. "I feel like I am experiencing an epiphany. Like never before, my sisters. It's like I have been speaking directly to God and he was answering my questions. He is telling me to stay strong and bonded to my partners and sisters. He kept using that word, sisters. And here we are again. Wondering what to do and seeking guidance."

Carla sat enchanted. She glanced around their luxurious suite at the wreckage from their last meal and called the front desk to ask for someone to come clean it up. She took a deep breath and closed her eyes for an eternity. Finally she spoke.

"Ladies, we are blessed here today. We have our love for each other which is undying and we have our love of God to keep us as one. One spirit, one entity. One force of nature if we can stay on the right path. I'm not sure yet what that path is or what it will involve but I know there is a path here for us. I know this in my heart. And I know that my love for you is binding and permanent. Sarah darling, am I making any sense? Can you feel my heart beating for you and the others? Can you see what I see for us in our future?"

Sarah squatted on the floor, her legs crossed over at her knees. Her eyes were closed but they could tell she was wide awake. Finally she opened them and smiled that Sarah smile that they all longed for every day. Her lips trembled as she clasped her hands together. The rings she wore were chosen by Melody. Gorgeous, broken Melody. Their tigress. The worst of them and sometimes the best. This is what made her so fascinating. She had gotten a new tattoo in Charleston at a well known parlor. It was a tiger holding a rose with a bleeding heart beside it. At last she rose to speak, struggling to regain her composure. They all knew she would. She was Melody the Magnificent.

"With all my faith in God I stand before you, afraid and but also brave. I think when we sing together it is magic. I think we all need magic at this precious time. I believe in us with all my heart."

Sarah kept a book of prayers in her pocket, some of which included the score. She learned to read music as a child when her parents taught her the violin and cello. She turned the pages slowly to one of her favorites and sang to her sisters.

There's a garden where Jesus is waiting,
There's a place that is wondrously fair.
For it glows with the light of His presence,
'Tis the beautiful garden of prayer.
O the beautiful garden, the garden of prayer,
O the beautiful garden of prayer.
There my Savior awaits, and He opens the gates
To the beautiful garden of prayer.
There's a garden where Jesus is waiting,
And I go with my burden and care.
Just to learn from His lips, words of comfort,
In the beautiful garden of prayer.
There's a garden where Jesus is waiting,
And He bids you to come meet Him there,
Just to bow and receive a new blessing,
In the beautiful garden of prayer.

A gentle knock got only Carla's attention. She turned her head toward it and Sarah thought that only a parrot or an owl could twist its neck like that. The knock grew more insistent. Finally Carla got up and stepped barefooted toward the door. The sweater she wore over little else was too suggestive but she stopped at the door. As the knock grew more insistent, Carla asked "who's there?" Silence greeted her pretty pale face, seating those electrifying green eyes. She asked again and the voice responded, "Security." She held her breath for a moment and asked again who was there. Again, he answered "Security" and asked her to please open the door.

Against her better judgment, Carla opened the door. In front of her stood the most handsome man she ever seen with gigantic delivery of flowers. All her favorites from the south. Against her better judgment she let him in.

"Hello young lady, I'm Jim. These are for you. From a special admirer of you and your team." Carla accepted the gift, an enormous vase of southern flowers. Blue false indigo, with its delicate beautiful purple blooms, black tupelo, moonglow sweetbay magnolias, shooting stars, and even blue shadow magnolias. All spiked with fresh lavender spikes, laced in perfectly. Carla stood mesmerized, inhaling the fragrance deep into her lungs.

Carla thanked him and turned to place them on the table. She saw a tiny card and ripped it open.

"Hello Miss Carla, I am a close friend of someone you know very well. She told me that you might appreciate this little gift. A hope they find you well." A tiny piece of paper lay folded in the card. Hooked, she opened it. "I so want to be your friend. You can trust me. I just have one favor to ask, if it pleases you. If you could ever fall in love with someone like me, it would make me the happiest man on earth. I would be your slave. Your love slave no matter what happened to us. Someone who would love you forever for all you are, not for what you seem to be, for your essence and not for your appearance." Carla wondered why this part was printed. She thought it looked like Times New Roman, one of her favorite fonts.

Carla sat entranced by this stranger from another land. She could not help fantasizing about him when Jim disgorged a small canister and pulled a charger. Joanna, Melody, Brandy, Sarah and Michelle sat in awe, not just from the flowers but from watching Carla melt in front of them. They had never seen her react quite this way, especially over a man, if it was really a man.

In an instant, the aromatic bouquet from heaven gave way to a peculiar smell. Not like the gas in her condo, this was not hydrogen sulfide, that was for sure. Joanna spoke first. "Hey, do y'all smell something funny? It sure isn't those flowers."

Carla knew they were in danger but could hardly speak. Finally she gasped, "Get out ladies. We are being attacked. Get out this second or we will die in our reverie. Forget the hell divers, forget about me, just get out the door. That's an order ladies!"

They were still racing out the door when the concussion from hell exploded. Carla looked back at poor Sarah, pulling up the rear. It didn't look good.

BLITZ

"What cruel mistakes are sometimes made by benevolent men and women in matters of business about which they know nothing and think they know a great deal... Rather, ten times, die in the surf, heralding the way to a new world, than stand idly on the shore."

- Florence Nightingale

The smelly fire bomb accelerated the ladies' burst out the door at the elegant Four Seasons. Only Brandy had not managed to get out in time. Her mangled legs and torso shocked Carla into a netherworld of Iraq and Afghanistan. The rest of her team lay in a tangled heap against the wall in the corridor. A renaissance print in a heavy frame crashed onto Joanna's head. Twisting her neck in pain, she saw what lay behind them through Carla's practiced eyes and rose to help her grab Brandy under her arms and lift her out to join them.

Brandy reminded them of soldiers critically wounded in an IED attack. Her blood sprayed around them as if from a runaway carwash, they figured her for dead but would never leave a fallen fellow soldier behind. The ladies made their way to the nearest elevator and rode down eleven flights in abject terror. The young red headed concierge with an adolescent mustache who greeted them in the lobby began to vomit. Several other guests soon joined in. Only one had the presence of mind to call 911. In minutes they heard sirens wailing and soon saw a fleet of ambulances and police squad cars approaching. Carla stood ready to meet them.

The first man through the door was a uniformed sergeant. Identifying himself as Tom Bailey, he methodically introduced three other officers. Bailey begin slowly and calmly.

"Ladies, whatever happened just now may have been the work of professionals. Possibly organized crime. I'm sending two of my men upstairs to check out the scene and will alert the medics where to go. There is an ambulance outside, actually three of them, and they will be taking you to Boston Medical Center. All of you. Once you are all stable, I will come visit you to take your statement and whatever other information your friends may have to offer. You may start now, if you like, as the medics come in and load everyone up on stretchers. I realize you may be traumatized right now and have every right to be. So I can wait to see you in the hospital before we talk in any detail. A forensics team will also be upstairs shortly and they are very thorough and professional. Several of them have served in combat, and one of them has two purple hearts. They are the best at what they do. Conway and Britton. I've known them for many years in this job.

BMC at One Boston Medical Center Place, was built a century ago, and grew its stellar reputation on the finest in advanced medical treatment and patient care. Its community outreach program had been serving the local homeless population for many years. On any given day, as at Mass General Hospital, the sad dirty faces of area down and outs were passed virtually unnoticed by the unceasing parade of patients, visitors and staff. Michelle remembered seeing the same elderly woman slumped over in a wheelchair outside the entrance for days. Same filthy throwaway clothes, same scrawny build. Same underweight creature barely as heavy as a suitcase. She gave her a twenty one day and the woman accepted it meekly while barely looking up. She mumbled something which Michelle took for a thankyou before returning to her stupor.

Michelle's friend Dan asked why she handed over the cash knowing that she might spend it on alcohol or drugs. "And what the hell if she does?" answered Michelle. Maybe it will make her happy for a little while, what's wrong with that and besides, I'm not her mother. Get a grip, Dan." That ended the conversation and they headed in the door. Dan silently agreed that he deserved that kick in the butt.

BMC is a private, 514-bed, academic medical center nestled in Boston's historic South End. It stands proud as "the largest safety-net hospital and busiest trauma and emergency services center in New England."

Its website proclaims, *"For more than 100 years, Boston Medical Center has been driven by a commitment to care for all people, providing not only traditional medical care, but also programs and services that wrap around that care to enhance overall health. All of this supports our mission to provide exceptional care, without exception."* Carla and her comrades felt assured they were in the right place. They desperately needed exceptional.

Their round the clock care went on for days, then a week. Their traumatic injuries retreated by the hour. The nursing staff was angelic, looking in on them repeatedly. Their attending physician, Tony Branden, was tall, Hollywood handsome with a kind look that made them feel special. Worshipped. Melody and Sarah felt they might be falling in love. Even Carla, String Bean herself, Carla the

Great, began to share the same feelings. They began to fantasize about sharing a life together. How many bedrooms would they need? Let society be damned.

Carla and her crew spent 10 days in the hospital. Eventually they grew to like the food, but only after barely eating the first three days. The nurses stopped administering morphine after the second day. Massachusetts physicians were reluctant to administer narcotics unless absolutely essential. Carla was not considered essential and received nothing but Tylenol and ibuprofen. These did nothing but the self-proclaimed top broad on the East Coast silently grit her teeth and waited for the doctor to come back in. He arousing feelings she had not experienced in years. Her electric green eyes kept him riveted. He could feel his heart quicken whenever he entered her room. This is not professional, he thought. Not even close. God help me.

Sarah spent two days in the intensive care unit, overseen by spine and orthopedic specialists. Twice, a diminutive psychiatrist named Fritz Zellinger, came in to evaluate her and make sure she was taking her antipsychotic meds. He watched as she swallowed them with orange juice and assured her she would be fine. While under morphine, Sarah felt better than fine. She had never felt so relaxed, calm, so at peace with herself. She watched a British soccer game on television and imagined that she married one of the goalies. Occasionally she would gasp, imagining them in bed together. She wasn't crazy about his jersey colors, but figured they could be dispensed with as she stripped him naked. The morphine still kicking in, she saw herself in a luxurious wedding dress, white orchids circling her head. This was her first glimpse of heaven and that itself was addictive.

November 11, Veterans Day. Chief nurse Karen Foley brought their discharge papers. Carla reached for a pen and began to sign. She asked about the other girls, as she called them. They began to answer through the hallway when the emergency lights on the floor began to flash and a siren wailed. Now who the hell was torturing them?

LAST RODEO

Carla, Joanna, Melody, Brandy, and Sarah hunkered down back in the Four Seasons hotel. As always, fresh flowers adorned the windowsills and tables. The gardenias were intoxicating. Especially for Sarah, whose mental illness was barely kept in check by her new meds. As always she sat in a wing chair, her hands now clasped in her lap. She was as lovely as ever, wrinkles kept in check by a concoction of creams that Melody picked up around Boston. Sarah looked wistfully out a window, not wishing to speak. Carla and Joanna knew what that meant.

They had returned to the hotel joyous and free again. Free from their injuries and their trauma. Their discharge had been marred, temporarily disrupted by a kitchen fire in the hospital cafeteria and a propane leak on the floor where they were all being treated. Security personnel responded quickly, sealing off the leak and extinguishing a grease fire. Huge industrial fans were brought in to blow the gas out three windows at the end of the hall. Carla's pretty print dress, a lovely creation from TripIit, blew above her thighs reminding Joanna of the famous photo of Marilyn Monroe standing over an air vent in Manhattan. She had to laugh, thinking that Carla had much better legs. Longer for sure.

The Four Seasons maintenance department made quick work out of the disaster in Carla's former suite. They went all out and in 48 hours replaced the carpet, re-wallpapered the walls, and installed all new furniture and decor. Fred Carlson, the general manager, told them the suite looked better than ever.

The gang convened with the boss. As always, fresh flowers adorned the windowsills and tables. The gardenias were intoxicating. Especially for Sarah, whose mental illness was barely kept in check by her new meds. As always she sat in a wing chair, her hands now clasped in her lap. She was as lovely as ever, wrinkles kept in check buy a concoction of creams that Melody picked up around Boston. Sarah looked wistfully out the window, not wishing to speak. Carla and Joanna knew what that meant.

"Well, girls we got lucky," began Carla. "Again. If God is not looking after us, then I am a baboon pulling his wanger in the jungle." "A really pretty one, boss," teased Joanna. Carla flashed that classic smile of hers, perfect teeth setting off her glorious green eyes, piercing through her team as they always had.

She turned open the Bible that has been placed in the room and began to read from Romans 8:38-39. No one had the temerity to respond while she spoke. Brandy had quietly put on Yo-Yo Ma playing *Ave Maria*. The luscious classic bathed them in a sea of reunion and redemption.

> *"For I am convinced that neither death nor life, neither angels nor demons, neither the present nor the future, nor any powers, neither height nor depth, nor anything else in all creation, will be able to separate us from the love of God that is in Christ Jesus our Lord."*

"So like I said before, my fellow cowgirls, we need to move on. We need to go back to Charleston and continue our path to redemption. We are going to dedicate our lives to helping and supporting those in need. No more blowing up thanks, no more robbing auctions, no more death and destruction. We know how to do this, we know how to march into greatness but also into humility. Actually, I believe it will be our humility that fuels our greatness for however long God sees fit to hold us together. We will be back to Charleston tomorrow my brave warrior cowgirls. In lovely transcendent Charleston we will begin our last rodeo."